THE BRITTLE
AGE

Donatella Di Pietrantonio

THE BRITTLE AGE

Translated from the Italian
by Ann Goldstein

Europa
editions

Europa Editions
8 Blackstock Mews
London N4 2BT
www.europaeditions.co.uk

A catalogue record for this title is available from the British Library
ISBN 978-1-78770-561-6

Di Pietrantonio, Donatella
The Brittle Age

Cover design by Ginevra Rapisardi

Prepress by Grafica Punto Print – Rome

The authorized representative in the EEA
is Edizioni e/o, via Gabriele Camozzi 1, 00192 Rome, Italy.

Printed and bound in Great Britain by Clays Ltd, Elcograf S.p.A

CONTENTS

To all the women who survive

There is no such thing as a natural death:
nothing that happens to man is ever natural,
since his presence calls the world into question.
—SIMONE DE BEAUVOIR, *A Very Easy Death*

THE BRITTLE AGE

AMANDA

1.

The mess I find in the morning reminds me that I'm not alone anymore. Amanda's back. I look around and stumble on her traces: on the arm of the sofa the plate with a torn-up slice of bread, in the glass the remains of a drink. The blanket is heaped in a corner, next to the book that's always turned over onto the same page.

Lately, my sleep has grown heavier, I don't hear her moving around the house. Only occasionally, when I turn on one side, her late-night steps vibrate as far as the floor of my room.

I don't know what time she'll wake up. I drink my coffee and put the biscotti on the table, along with the only cup left from her adolescence. The sun coming through the window falls on it, lights up the cow with a tuft of grass in its mouth.

I leave the empty pitcher on the stove, a signal that says: warm the milk. She can pour in the coffee left in the coffeepot or ignore it all. She can appreciate my care for her or bristle at being treated like a child.

I don't understand her shifts at work, if I can call it that: her comings and goings are unpredictable. Any question I ask on the subject irritates her. I try to run into her at meals.

I make sure there's something nourishing in the fridge, in case she skips breakfast. The perfect shells of the eggs reassure me. She's always thin, my daughter.

I pick up the shoes and slippers from the rug, I clear off the sofa. If someone should arrive, I'd be embarrassed to let the room be seen like this. Amanda's phone under the blanket is dead.

I can leave. Today I'm going to see her grandfather, I write on a piece of paper. I put it near the vase of yellow tulips. I add a heart, and immediately erase it.

My father lives halfway between the town and the mountain. He's not in the fields: this morning he's sitting near the hearth, out of sorts. Time passes slowly for him at home; reading a page of the newspaper tires him and TV is all chatter.

"There's a place I have to take you," he says.

The day is so clear it almost wounds us. He's never worn sunglasses, he squeezes his eyelids when a ray dazzles him. We're winding uphill in his old Brava, curve after curve. One of my ears pops, then the other, and the engine sounds louder. He's intent on driving, his profile jolts with every pothole in the asphalt, his nose gets sharper, his lips sucked in. At a certain point he rouses himself, asks about Amanda.

"She was sleeping," I say, and we're silent.

Before us is the mountain. The new green is moving upward, it colors the age-old beech grove and what the shepherds call the *nudo*, where no trees grow and the open land stretches into the distance. Beyond the open land it's still winter.

Gradually the road becomes more familiar to him; he's walked it countless times, when it was unpaved, or only a path. He could be driving now with his eyes closed. He looks out the window: he was born down there, in the strip of cultivated fields, and twenty-five years later I was born. He was a young man in this valley, I only a child. Then we moved to where he lives now. Here he hunted, sometimes poached.

It's a long time since we've been to the mountain together,

how long I can't calculate. He opens the window a little, breathes deeply. He forgets the emphysema and the aortic stenosis, his hollow cheeks swell. He's always missed the air he left here.

We reach his goal, he parks on the side of the road.

The Sheriff's *casotto*, a crude cabin, is still standing, even without her. I remember when I used to sit with the hikers at the tables in the field, in the smoke of the *arrosticini,* the meat grilling on skewers. Or helped serve, if I was needed.

The leaves of the beeches, unfurling, just graze the roof.

"This piece of woods is still ours, keep that in mind for afterward," says my father and points to his family's original property.

"Afterward" is when he is no longer here. I can make an application to the forest service and cut wood for the winter, he explains. He knows I won't do it: he's never found a fire lighted in my house.

"Did you bring me here to leave me the woods?" I joke.

"It's not only what you see."

He crosses the road and turns onto a path invaded by weeds. I follow his painful steps reluctantly, I know what's over there.

I didn't remember the camping sign looking like this: it's lost some letters, and the M is hanging upside down, becoming a W. A spray of brambles twines around the gate, closed with a padlock; I didn't know he had a key. He forces the gate open, conquering the friction of iron bars against the overgrown earth, walks toward the few brick walls, crumbling with neglect. Under a roof the row of sinks for the campers, some vandalized, like the ripped-off doors of the toilets. We skirt the long side of the pool, he always a few steps ahead. Amid garbage and broken branches on the ground a sapling grows, uncertain, twisted. Farther along, you can no longer distinguish the spaces cleared for the tents; they've been repossessed by the vegetation.

"Tell me why we've come here—who gave you the key?"

"I wanted to show you how derelict the place is."

I shrug. I've seen it, and we can go. The place doesn't interest me.

"This, too, becomes yours, afterward," he says.

An alarm signal rises from my stomach to my throat, suffocating me.

"That's impossible. You sold this land."

He tried for a long time, he confesses, without success.

I'm silent for a while, in the chorus of birds. At regular intervals the cuckoo solos.

"After what happened no one wanted it, I couldn't give it away," he says, as if to justify himself.

"I don't want it, either, it's a frightening place."

I've raised my voice, the last syllables echo. It will be mine of necessity, I'm his only heir.

"One of these days we'll go to the notary and settle it."

That is the power my father still holds over me, decisions already made that I can't change.

"I won't accept it, I have enough to worry about."

I turn my back and head toward the car. I no longer hear calls of love from the woods. All this April rebirth doesn't concern me.

Milan or nothing. So she said of her future, the last year of high school. The town—staying here—was nothing. Milan: the city where life would really happen for her.

She prepared all summer: I found her on the bed in the afternoon, one pencil stuck in her pulled-back hair and another marking x's on the tests. She barely went out, and then reluctantly: those who texted or called were the past.

She didn't even listen to my proposals: Rome was too close, Bologna provincial.

"Then why are your friends going there?"

"They've got no guts—they stop at a safe distance."

At a shopping center we chose one big suitcase and one small. She wanted them to be strong, even if she would return only at Christmas and Easter, she told me.

"You'll come see me sometimes, it'll be good for you," she answered the silent objections of my gaze.

In September her father took her to the University of Milan for the admissions exam. Amanda called me before she went in. In her voice a mixture of fear and determination that I knew.

She returned with the lights of the city in her eyes.

"It's like being in Europe," she said.

They had stopped for dinner in the Navigli. It had been a kind of tourist trip, I understood from the little she told. She was radiant, after two days spent with her father.

"What you make isn't a true Milanese cutlet," and she put a pitying hand on my shoulder.

When she told her grandfather she had been accepted he opened a bank account with a thousand euros. "Every time I collect my pension I'll put in fifty or a hundred," he promised.

It seemed to him impossible that she could withdraw it from so far away. And mysterious what she would study: international relations and European institutions. But he had heard her commenting on the newscast, with that rebellion in her voice.

My father was proud of his only granddaughter, thirty-second out of more than four hundred on the entrance exam. It had been an effort for him, at first, to accept the newborn's coloring, the almost pink hair that didn't belong to our family.

I, too, was proud of her ranking on the exam. I had silenced in myself a half hope that she wouldn't pass. A small serpent hidden in a deep cave wanted to keep her.

I bought her new sheets and towels, pajamas, all the necessities that girls don't think of. In a few days I taught her to load the washing machine, hang the dark clothes out to dry in the shade. She would discover a little of the world that hadn't been possible for me.

I went with her on the train; the suitcases were heavy.

"We could have at least bought the sheets in Milan, couldn't we?" she said.

But they were light, compared with the jars of sauce. Those were enough for months. I had cooked for the long term. Only with that exercise was I convinced that she could survive without me.

The elevator was broken. We sweated together up the building's rather gloomy stairs. The girl who opened the door examined Amanda and pointed to her room.

"Afterward come in here and sign the contract," she said.

The other roommates didn't appear. The room had a shabby dresser, dust had accumulated in the corners. Amanda didn't seem to notice. She let me stay only long enough to help her arrange some things in the closet.

"I'm going to the bathroom," I said before calling a taxi and leaving.

I sat on the toilet; the floor tiles were so dirty. But they weren't exactly dirty, only too old. In the tub was a plastic curtain with a pattern of little elephants, the schedule for cleaning was fixed to the door. A question mark was waiting to be replaced by Amanda.

The taxi would take me back to the station. I hugged her hard. "Call when you get home," Amanda said, freeing herself.

It was the first time she had said that to me.

4.

A year and a half later my daughter took one of the last trains. After that you couldn't leave Milan or any other place in Italy. I looked at the TV coverage of people rushing up the escalators, crowding onto the platforms. I also searched for her, the flame of her hair in the throng. Meanwhile she spoke to me on the phone: Maybe I'll manage to get on. I imagined her making her way, so tiny, with the suitcase. They were all returning to the south.

She arrived at ten at night, two hours late. Unloading the suitcases took an endless time: a boy was handing them down from the baggage car. He got out to smoke half a cigarette before departing again.

Instinctively I approached, she stopped me with her hand. It could be dangerous, she said.

In the car she turned on the radio and fell back against the seat, letting her head loll as if she were sleeping. She was too tired to talk, apart from the minimum.

"Why did you carry all that weight?" I asked. "In a few weeks the emergency will be over, the universities will reopen."

"What do you know about it? You can't predict."

She looked distractedly at the gateway into the town, the benedictory saint in the niche.

At home I turned on the oven to warm the pasta for her; she turned it off.

"I'll eat tomorrow."

She went into her room with the backpack, the rest remained in the living room. Behind her door I heard not a sound.

Later I opened the suitcases, there were the colored sheets I had bought for her. With the cotton in my hands I had a presentiment that there was something obscure and definitive in that return.

In the morning I let her sleep. She was recovering from the strain of the trip. But she hadn't eaten. And the day before there hadn't been time even for a sandwich before getting on the train. The café service on board had been suspended.

I began to count the hours, as when she was a baby and wouldn't wake to be fed. Then when she woke she'd have a fierce hunger, and bit my nipples with her sharp gums.

Bringing up Amanda was painful. I didn't understand her, I didn't understand what she wanted from me. I was afraid of being alone with her. At night my husband put her on his shoulder and carried her around the house, after closing the bedroom door to let me sleep.

The other mothers in the pediatrician's waiting room recognized the cause as soon as their child wailed. My daughter was crying and I didn't know why. My breasts were full, and yet sometimes she pulled away and screamed. The milk must not be good, I thought. I squeezed some on a finger and licked it. Maybe what tasted sweet to me became bitter on her small tongue. I remember that I shook her to make her stop crying, though not too hard.

Twenty years later a new worry gripped me while Amanda wouldn't wake up. Eleven o'clock, twelve. Maybe in Milan she had taken night for day as when she was an infant. I began moving around the house noisily, banging pans, shifting furniture. Only Rubina noticed.

From the balcony below she heard me: come down, she said with a gesture. She was sitting on a chaise, her skirt pulled high on her thighs and her sleeves rolled up.

I also arranged myself for the March sun.

"Amanda's back, you hung out her clothes."

She asked me how she was, and I didn't know. Tired, I answered. "She'll study here at home for a while."

She nodded, eyes closed. But I hadn't found any books in her suitcases.

"Now we're forced to rest, to come to a halt," said Rubina, turning her arms to the whiter side.

She was sorry about the suspension of choir practice.

"The last few times we'd got freer with the Gypsy song," and she hummed the start.

I had no wish to talk, I was only waiting for my daughter to get up. Every so often I looked surreptitiously at my watch. "I'm going up," I said at one-thirty.

At home, with the sun still in my eyes, I couldn't see clearly. I knocked on her door, then entered. She was under the covers, her head hidden by the pillow. I uncovered her face, for a moment she looked at me as if she didn't recognize me.

"I'm in quarantine, get away," she said. "I'll eat in my room."

"We can sit at the two ends of the table, it's long enough."

She sat up, grim.

I aired the room while she served herself a plate of gnocchi in the kitchen. As soon as she finished she shut herself in again.

That night, toward dawn, a soft movement on the other side of the bed woke me. Amanda was curled up, making herself small and round, her back turned toward me. I don't know how long I lay there without moving, surprised. Then she started crying. Without sound, only sobs and sniffling. I encircled her as much as I could, my arms light. "Don't ask me anything," she said.

That was the last time I was so close to my daughter. It was scarcely more than a year ago.

5

I n those weeks Amanda slept. She during the day, I at night, owl and lark. We lived in the common rooms by turns and every so often collided.

Around noon I'd be gripped by a frenzy for waking her in some way. I ran the vacuum cleaner for a long time in the hall in front of her room, as if all the dirt in the house were concentrated there. I knew it was useless, but maybe the sound at its highest level would suggest to her, in sleep, that outside her closed eyelids and the room was the light of spring, of life.

"You simply have to get up," I shouted once.

She uncovered half of her head, a moment. A rheumy gaze.

"And after that what do I do?"

I offered a list: eat, study, a walk in the neighborhood or a little exercise.

She answered point by point. "I'm not hungry. I don't have books. Exercise is useful to you because you're in menopause."

The stale smell of her mouth, which was always closed, remained in the air. I grabbed the edge of the sheet and with a tug pulled it off, exposing her shape huddled in pajamas with a pattern of paired cherries.

She got up abruptly, pushed me hard. The wardrobe supported me. I didn't want to fall.

"Don't ever try that again," I said, my sweaty palms on the door.

She sat on the bed. Under the lamp that she left burning at night, the mass of her hair was opaque, all the shadings of red without luster.

"You've got to wash, you smell bad."

She didn't react. We remained like that for a while, I standing before her. Rage descended slowly, inflaming faces. We were taking the measure of each other in order not to become enemies.

Her phone rang somewhere under the bed. I'd heard it before, over and over. My wordless question: why don't you answer. The phone absorbed the rings, one after another, then a message arrived.

"Breakfast is still there, lunch, too," I said. It was three in the afternoon.

Later water ran in the bath and I felt a relief near joy. So she listened, every so often. I still had a chink to whisper through.

I opened the window in her room, fresh air burst into the disorder. I reached an arm under the bed, fearful of being surprised. Some Lorenzo had called several times, and also her father. I pushed the phone back to where it had been.

From the bathroom the sound of running water and then the dryer, reassuring me. Here's what I had come to: a mother happy to hear that her daughter was bathing. She emerged sweet-smelling, her hair falling like a cloud over her chest; her eyes, streaked with brown, seemed greener. She didn't shut herself in her room, but she disappeared.

As I answered her father I tried to remember how long it had been since he called me.

"What's going on?" he asked.

He was worried, he hadn't spoken to her on the phone for weeks.

"If that's your worry, she doesn't talk to me, either," I said. "Or to anyone else."

"But what does she do in the house?"

"Nothing."

"And you can't budge her?"

I couldn't, no, and still can't. He was welcome to come and

try if he thought he could. On that occasion I would bring up again certain questions that he no longer even remembered. And maybe he would take the sweaters he'd left in the closet. They're still there. Sometimes I pull them out, for fear of moths. I spread them against the light to see if there are any holes. There aren't, the wool is high-quality. I refold them and put them back, in two piles.

"I can't move," said Dario.

And so I couldn't help him.

My father is angry with me for not filing divorce papers. Neither you nor that wimp, he grumbles. It's true, this omission binds us, along with other things we don't know. Amanda, of course.

I still find myself embarrassed if I have to name him. "Husband" clashes in my mouth, "ex-husband" doesn't work, "father of my daughter," I don't know.

Then, from the balcony, I saw Amanda. Rubina was combing her hair with one hand and with the other cutting it. They were in the sun, in the garden. A little, just a little: Amanda restrained her, showing her a couple of centimeters between thumb and index finger. Only the split ends.

6.

My father offered a Mass, as he's done every May since he was widowed. A week before, he puts on his glasses and looks up Don Arturo in an old address book, written by my mother's quick hand, how long ago who can say. He sets the date and then informs close relatives, whose phone numbers he knows by heart. Last he calls me.

It's more important this time, after the disappointment of the previous year. "Remember her only in your heart," the priest consoled him at a distance. He was offended; he remembers her every day without needing someone to suggest it.

On the phone he talks about the garden, we negotiate over the tomato plants to put in, but he has already decided to plant more than two hundred, as usual. It's his defiance of age, of illness.

"Bring Amanda to church," he says at the end.

So he shifts me in a moment from the damp earth that welcomes roots and seeds to my most painful point.

"I don't know if she's working Thursday afternoon," I warn him.

"That's a job?" he asks. "If necessary she can get time off, for her grandmother."

Amanda uses the pretext that I had already used, no one can take her shift at the café.

She doesn't want to come. She won't submit to the looks of relatives she cares nothing about. The only gaze that can wound her is her grandfather's, and she'll avoid it.

I try to insist at another moment, meeting her at the door to the bathroom. That's where I plan my ambushes.

"But if even you don't believe in these Masses," she says with an expression both compassionate and contemptuous.

My father sees me get out of the car alone and doesn't comment. He chats with the priest in front of the church. It's one of the few churches still open in the countryside, concrete and brick, from the seventies. It repulses me every time.

"I don't know how to advise you, Don Artu', I don't know about that stuff."

Don Arturo's been growing truffles in a small plot he owns.

We all sit at the proper distance, he and I in front. He turns to see who's there and who isn't.

Above the altar I find the two groups of crudely frescoed angels with a blazing God at the center. I miss the smell of incense and I miss my mother, for the time of this celebration in her memory. Maybe she'd know how to help me with Amanda.

My mother died every day, month, and year of her illness. One by one her abilities disappeared: cooking for twenty people at the harvest, copying an embroidery from a needlework magazine, smiling at her only grandchild.

"Signora, would you like to buy a rabbit?" she asked me when we'd already lost her.

She left my father last: she stopped calling him. For a long time I hadn't been a single person to her. I was always changing, from a lady who was buying a rabbit to a thief who was stealing money from the drawer of the night table.

Today she would look at us with tenderness, husband and daughter, alone in the first row, each with our own pain locked in our chest. She would take our hands to comfort us. I try to imagine the warmth of her clasp.

In the sermon Don Arturo lavishes words on the active woman she was, always at her husband's side. I don't know if, in the full possession of her faculties, she would have wanted to be remembered like that. A tireless worker, the priest repeats, slightly bombastic. He's pleased with this reassuring and partial truth. He doesn't know that in order to rest my mother had to get sick. Before, her husband gave her no respite, he wanted her to be a man in the countryside, a woman in the house.

The Mass is endless, the way it seemed to me as a girl. I don't join in the chorus of the prayers, I don't cross myself or take communion or kneel. Hymns are banned, and anyway I've never liked the church hymns. Sometimes I liked the voices, but the adoring devotion of the texts disturbed me. Don Arturo tolerates my detached presence, maybe he still hopes that his words will convert me. I stand and sit with the others, however. I also used to hold out my hand to my neighbors; now we don't exchange the sign of peace, we only look at one another. I hadn't seen our old family doctor, behind us. He came, too, for my mother. I could talk to him about my daughter, but I don't know what to say about her. Maybe that she's apathetic about everything.

At the Our Father I breathe with relief, soon we'll go in peace.

Outside we greet the relatives and some people from the neighborhood, without touching them; a friend of my mother's waits a little apart until the others leave. She can't resist and hugs me. They knew each other as girls, went together to the nuns, learned to embroider. Then she married a man from the town: she had an easier life.

"What about Amanda, what's she doing?" she asks with that affectionate anxiety to hear great results.

"For now she's studying at home," I lie. "She found a part-time job, that's why she's not with us."

"I remember her in her grandmother's arms, she was her joy."

My father and I remain on this black paved area in front of

the church, Don Arturo locks the church and joins us. Each of us wants to give him thirty euros for the Mass, my father gets his way. He hands him the bills holding them hidden in his fist, as if they were a little obscene.

"That was a nice sermon you gave for Concetta," he thanks him as he says goodbye.

Then we head to the cars and he tells me he's made an appointment with the notary, on the day my office is closed. He doesn't even leave me the time to get angry.

"See what you want to do about your daughter. I stopped to have a coffee in that café earlier, and she wasn't there."

7.

I look for her on the screen and find people like her. The withdrawn. Shut in their rooms, in their heads. M. didn't leave the house for three years. He and his mother talk about it in a video, sitting in blue armchairs. Come to us, here, I'd like to say to the expert with the well-groomed mustache who comments afterward. Come and talk in front of Amanda's door, maybe she'll open it to you. Maybe she'll give your know-it-all face a reason.

The Japanese, on the other hand, study the plasma. They compare altered levels of some amino acids, of bilirubin. Maybe she's sick, then. She's so thin, pale. Some days her eye sockets are dark as bruises, in the little I see her. At the table she wants the television on, in order not to feel the silence, the weight of my gaze. She eats a few bites, then gets up and goes to her room, though she just came out. In those minutes my appetite, too, is distracted, diminishes.

She comes back and sits down and stares at the plate, stretches one leg out on the chair. She starts again, the pasta is already tepid and now she doesn't like it. She twists her mouth and forces herself to finish, maybe she gets up once or twice more. If I ask her to get a bottle of water or some silverware from the drawer, it costs her an effort. And yet she's been awake for half an hour.

Digestion seems to drain all her energy, and she drops onto the sofa. She runs her thumb over the phone without interest. She fights me with muteness and negatives: each of her sentences contains at least one. There are moments when she's suddenly yielding. I take advantage, persuade her, drive her to the hospital for blood tests.

A nurse welcomes us, she's kind, we know each other. Amanda goes to the exam room, the nurse's hand on her shoulder. She's upset by the needles, they'll keep her for a few minutes.

I have nothing to read in the waiting room. At this moment the nurse will have tightened the strap, she'll be tapping the vein to prick. Amanda's veins are mobile and deep, hard to find. The last time they had to search with the needles and she turned white. Maybe she's anemic, as I was at her age. My mother cooked me liver, got restoratives at the pharmacy.

A man comes out with the shirtsleeve rolled up on his left arm. I'm struck by his unhealthy color and something familiar in his slightly watery eyes. He also looks at me fleetingly, while he tries to fold the piece of paper he'll need to retrieve the report. It falls, I pick it up and hand it to him. Then his gaze revives.

"Hello, Osvaldo."

He stares at me and concentrates.

"I'm the daughter of—" but it's he who utters my father's name first.

"After all this time I didn't recognize you, with the mask," he says. "You've changed."

Not much remains of the man he was, either. But he's still so tall, he's maintained his straight back. I ask how he is, and he says so-so.

"It's not a good sign if you meet someone in the hospital."

He wants to know what I'm doing here.

"I brought my daughter."

Osvaldo throws the cotton in the garbage, rolls down his shirtsleeve, and buttons the wrist. We're not sure whether to say goodbye or exchange some more words.

"And it's a while since Doralice's been back?" I ask.

A slow slide of his head sideways, then he straightens it.

"Two and a half years. But I heard that the planes are starting to fly again," and he nods at the sky through the window.

Doralice, his daughter. I've seen her a few times since then, since she left, telling no one. I know that she seldom returns, and when she's here she stays with her parents in the country. A landslide narrowed the road that leads to the house, now only Osvaldo's old Ape can pass.

Doralice and I were girls together. At Amanda's age we saw each other almost every day. Maybe we wouldn't have become such close friends if our parents hadn't been. Most of all Osvaldo and my father.

When the camp was full of tourists, she worked at the *casotto* at night. At first her mother reproached her constantly: where'd you come from, Dorali'. With greasy hands Doralice picked up four or five glasses at a time, sticking her fingers in them. It was a casual place, but someone complained about the oily prints. She turned swiftly from table to table, dropping off carafes of wine and steaming trays. I liked helping her, all those people circulating. I was precise but slow. With you they'll die of hunger, Doralice said to me.

For the two of us, August was the most exciting month of the year. We met boys from other places, who'd disappear in a few days. After midnight the place emptied and we went behind the *casotto*, to drink cold beers. Inside we heard her mother finishing the cleanup, then counting the money.

One night, I remember, Doralice imitated that man who came from who knows where. Signorina, you don't have a side dish of plain spinach with butter? He hadn't left us a tip. Sitting on the empty crates we laughed raucously. She had a way of throwing her head back—it was one of the last times we laughed like that. Our youth was about to end, and we had no idea. Not even the somber cry of the owl worried us.

She doesn't want to be seen in the town, people said of her, after the crime. No one mentions her anymore now. They've all forgotten Doralice and her story. The young people of Amanda's age never knew her. Our parents didn't help us stay connected.

"The important thing is that she's OK where she is," Osvaldo consoles himself. "One of these days I'll go see your father. He called me."

Amanda hasn't eaten. I propose breakfast at the café near the hospital. We sit at a table outside.

Rubina says that with that sulky face she looks like the models of today. To me, in the crude morning light, she seems, rather, a vulnerable creature, barely emerged from a kingdom of shadows. She sips her cappuccino, tears off pieces of the cornetto and chews as if they were bitter.

I recognize Osvaldo's Ape pulled up on the sidewalk opposite, the same as then, only a little more faded. Mud spattered on the body. He hasn't left yet, I've no idea where he is.

Fragments of conversation from the other tables, a cheerfulness of spoons being put down. Here even a look from me can annoy her. I drink my coffee. I return silence with silence.

8.

A word from the director was enough to rouse the group: shall we start again? The chat suddenly became animated, everyone was asking when, where, sending smiley faces. It's been more than a year since the last meeting, and now we're free to have a rehearsal outdoors. Some proposed the lake, others a square; a scenic hill a few kilometers out of town was chosen.

Rubina parks behind the other cars and, scores under our arms, we walk toward the figures moving around the monumental oak. I look at them, and my heart unexpectedly beats faster.

She and I started singing on the way, wanting to hear if we still had a voice. We sang what Milo calls pop songs, not our repertory. At a stop sign the man in front stared at us in the rearview mirror, we'd entered through the window. Rubina laughed: when we're in the car she likes to imitate Thelma and Louise. In the past months no sound has come out of my mouth, while sometimes from her apartment vocalises have risen in crescendo or diminuendo, along with some choruses. My diaphragm was contracted, my breath short.

Samira sees us first, and comes toward us. Just a moment of hesitation, and I give her a hug, rediscover her scent. She's wearing a white dress, and her dark skin shows through the lace inserts: she looks almost like a bride. She's the only one from Pescara; she texted us, asking how to get here. The others are more cautious, greeting us at a distance, with a wave of their hands. They're standing in a wide circle, with Milo at the center. I didn't know how much I missed them. For now we keep our masks on.

"Welcome," and the director makes a little bow.

His eyes and his earlobe are shining. He turns around: scarcely more than half of us are present.

"I can understand the absent—they still don't feel safe," he says.

He's sorry there's not even one tenor, but we want to start again anyway. Outside it will be more difficult, he warns us, the voices get lost, they'll sound different. We arrange ourselves in two rows, not so close as before. Milo goes up to Rubina, speaks to her softly. Responding, she, so prudent, lowers her mask.

I plant my feet on the ground, relax my jaw. In the warmup vocalises I feel a little ridiculous without the protection of walls. Mi-o-o-o-o. The birds' chirping distracts me, they're gossiping on the ancient branches above our heads. Mi-o-o-o-o. The sound of steps running on gravel interrupts us, and we welcome Pierluigi with applause. He's still wearing his safety shoes and the shirt with the business logo. Now we have a tenor.

"Shall we try *Ederlezi* again?" Samira asks.

She likes the song, it's in her Romany language. For Milo it's too soon: we have to start with the pieces we've worked on longer.

"But we'll go back to it next week, to *Ederlezi*," he promises.

Of the directors who've succeeded one another over the years he's the most open. When I was a child the director seemed so old; before his misty eyes we sang only dialect songs and *Ave Maria*. We rehearsed in a bare room in the community center; in winter when we came out it was already night. The bus home was in the square, doors open and completely dark inside. The only journey I made was on that dilapidated bus. I'd get on—at that hour there was almost no one else, occasionally some shapes huddled on the back seats.

Doralice dreamed of going around the world; she laughed at me for being content with the same ten kilometers, continuously back and forth.

I came from the countryside, and the chorus connected me to the town. It's always had the town's name, that's its boast. One Christmas many years ago we even performed at the Vatican.

"Let's try *O magnum mysterium*," says the director.

I hesitate in this new beginning. We immediately shorten the meter's distance we'd imposed on ourselves; Milo pays no attention. I'm afraid of the others' breathing. The unpleasant breath of a bass behind me is alarming, it means we're too close.

A few minutes ago Rubina wasn't scared—she uncovered her face next to Milo's. I've never seen her so close to a man. It's years since her husband died; Giulio was just a child.

And I see myself, alone. I miss the familiarity, the intimacy of small daily habits. Sitting at the table across from the other, gazes meeting. This is the love I no longer have. It's become nostalgia.

With one hand cupped over my ear I try to find my voice. Outside our bodies, the space has become too vast to be pierced by a song. And yet the oak has a tremor, or am I imagining it.

Rubina is on my right, she's already been absorbed into the Virgin's womb. Without losing sight of the director, she turns slightly in my direction, touches my arm, encourages me with a tiny movement of her head. The power of the air she breathes out doesn't frighten me. She joined the chorus as an adult, but without her it would no longer exist.

I shift my hand to my throat, and now the vocal cords vibrate. I, too, enter the mystery. I've never experienced anything more like a religious feeling. The passage we know by heart sounds different in the changed world.

The time goes quickly, it's nearly dark now. Each of us folds up our instrument into ourself. In the cool of the evening

Samira puts on a red shawl. The phone flashlights are on and no one wants to leave. A bottle appears, nobody knows where the cork ended up. We dare to make a toast.

We drink prosecco and believe in a happy moment. I've forgotten about Amanda, about my father.

9.

He's waiting for us outside, sitting on a step in his cargo pants. He phoned his granddaughter and she answered. I don't know exactly what they said, about the land on the mountain, but it made her curious. At the table Amanda asked me why it's called Dente del Lupo, Wolf's Tooth. Maybe she wants to be forgiven for not going to the Mass.

Her grandfather tosses her the keys and takes the passenger seat. She hesitates for a moment, then sits behind the wheel. We start off, three generations heading for the ancient family property.

"Put it in second here," he advises her. "There's a tight curve."

The landscape has changed since the last time, what's blooming changes as we go up. Amanda sneezes, there's so much pollen in the air, even though she's not actually allergic. Her blood tests were perfect, even the iron is normal, although on the cusp. I expected an asterisk, and I was almost disappointed. I haven't yet discovered what's wrong with my daughter.

My father makes a sign to pull up near the drinking trough. We walk on the grass, he leads. His mouth grazes the spigot as he takes long cold sips.

"Mountain water restores you to the world," and he urges Amanda with a wave.

He'd also say that to me, when we brought the sheep here. I was a child, but I knew how to guide them with my cherry wood stick. I watched them while he went off with the gun over his shoulder, followed by Osvaldo. My father taught him to shoot, to hold still at the moment of the recoil. I stayed in this meadow while they tramped silently through the woods.

Later I heard their shots in the distance. Sometimes I fell asleep, leaning against the trough where the animals drank. My father returned with partridges hanging at his belt, heads dangling on his thigh. I hated him for the dead birds, the blood that stained his pants, the fear when I woke up alone. Maybe it wasn't even hate, at the age of eight.

He wanted a son, and I was born. My aunt left the room and said to him: don't get angry. A long time later he waited for a grandson, a child to put on the tractor. Together they would plow after the harvest, compress expanses of hay into round bales. My father was disappointed twice. His surname will die out with me, around here.

I didn't send my daughter to her grandparents in the summer. I imagined her in the garden in the sun, while he staked the tomato plants. I brought her to the environmental education center, which offered walks along the river, healthy snacks. At night Amanda told me she'd crossed the rope bridge and made bread. I kept her sheltered from her grandparents.

My father looks at the mountain, then at his granddaughter. "Dente del Lupo is up there," he tells her.

He'll wait for us here, he'll go see if that flock grazing at the end of the plain is Achille's. Amanda sets out on the old shepherds' path. She precedes me, flexible and light, and after a while takes off her sweatshirt and knots it around her waist.

We go into the beechwood, where it's almost dark at first, almost cold. A fallen tree, roots in the air, attached to a tangle of earth and rocks.

At a certain point the path forks, and she waits for me. I take the right. Where does the other direction go, Amanda asks. I don't know, I answer. A short stretch and we're out of the woods. We continue in the dry heat. The ascent is steeper, the stain of sweat expands on the back of her t-shirt. I'm panting, my heart beats rapidly, muscles that are out of practice strain. As a girl, I walked everywhere, out of necessity. My legs were thin but what strength!

This morning I underestimated Amanda's, now I follow her calm breathing. I don't want to delude myself about her. Tomorrow she'll shut herself in her room again, I know it.

Dente del Lupo now looms above us. The rock spur that gives its name to our family's woods and our land. A last effort and we stop beneath it. Some primeval earthquake expelled it from the center of the earth, so white. It's visible from every point of the valley: Doralice pointed that out to me. A year after the crime, more or less, she had found a job in a *birreria* at Quattro Strade. We hadn't seen each other. Hey, I said. She answered the same, it was our greeting. She was taking the last of the upside-down chairs off the tables. But when I asked how are you she was silent. We went outside, in the fading afternoon sun. I asked if she liked the job. It won't last long, she said. Later I understood that at that time she was unable to stay anywhere.

"Wherever I am, I always see it, do you?"

She pointed to the mountain, that white tooth that from a distance I couldn't distinguish.

"I see it at night, too, it shines on me."

I would have liked to apologize for all my failures, but I didn't have the words.

Tears rose, I held them back. She leaned on a low wall, looking at the landscape, restless.

"How green those fields are. But underneath the land's full of worms, it's rotten."

They called her from inside the bar, and that was how we parted that day, with the worms.

"It's true, it has the shape of a canine," Amanda says.

From two thousand meters we look at the valley, the city on the coast, and the sea. On the clearest days you can see the Croatian islands.

"There—what's that?" and she points below us, where the woods opens up for some roofs, the grayish rectangle of the old swimming pool.

"There used to be a campground. On your grandfather's property."

She wants to go see it, afterward. Sitting on the grass she bites into the sandwich with a hunger rediscovered. I show her a patch of *orapi* at our feet: wild spinach, good to eat.

"Why don't you like coming up here?" she asks.

"Who told you I don't like it?"

My father, certainly. He's silent or says the wrong thing. Now that I've cancelled the appointment with the notary he goes through her to reach me.

"He feels his age, he's worried about the future of his land," I say.

"It will be yours. He doesn't have other children."

It will be a burden for me, I think out loud. I should have gone away from here, I should have gone when I was young.

Amanda finishes the sandwich, crumples the napkin and puts it in her pocket.

"You always complain, but you chose to stay. No one forced you."

She drinks from the water bottle she filled at the trough.

"You weren't able to separate yourself," she concludes, "either before or after."

I'd like to answer that separating is complicated, and for her as well. She returned to the nothing that she wanted to leave. But then I look at the horizon, sky and water touch. And the villages perched on the hills. It's not nothing.

It's almost noon, and he must be tired, he must have talked a long time with Achille, if he's the shepherd of those sheep. We take a shortcut on the way down, skirting the snowfield: this warm May is eroding it, melting it drop by drop. Soon, they say, it will disappear.

Amanda wants to see the old campground. It's right around the bend, I can't escape. Can't cut short these hours when she's speaking to me.

"I don't have the key to the lock," I say in front of the gate.

She sets off along the edge of the enclosure, turns and sees me motionless. I obey her gesture of impatience.

"But was it Grandfather's?" she asks.

"Only the land. The campground was Osvaldo's."

She finds one of the iron stakes bent, the fence caved in. In a moment she's gone over it, not me.

"It's late, he's waiting for us," I remind her.

She holds out her hand and overcomes my resistance. She wanders through the desolation, touches the broken glass of a window with her foot. On the back of the toilets she discovers some writing, in red paint faded by the years: on one side, KILL HIM, and on the other, on two lines, VIRGINIA AND TANIA ALIVE FOR EVER.

"What does that mean?"

"It happened long ago, before you were born. A crime."

"But where?" she presses me.

"In the woods. At Pietra Rotonda, at the end of that path we didn't take."

She's silent for a few moments. She looks again at the writing, then at me.

"Who were Virginia and Tania? Did you know them?"

"Only by sight."

"And Grandfather was here?"

"No, not him, Osvaldo."

But Grandfather hasn't slept for years, I tell her. He still sometimes dreams gunshots that wake him in the night.

10.

Rubina has left the door slightly ajar for me. I got a message from her a little while ago, and I put the olives she needed on the counter. The filet of baccalà is already cut in pieces, she's flouring it. Certain dishes don't work if you cook only a single portion, she says. I bring her whatever's ripe from my father's garden. Today, too, I brought her a head of lettuce. She browns the onion in the earthenware pot, then she puts it aside.

"And Amanda?" she asks.

"A guest showed up, a boy."

She looks at me and continues with the sequence of ingredients that are sautéed, then removed.

"And why aren't you pleased?"

"I don't know, it's the first time I've seen him, but I don't like him."

I found them at the window, talking, when I got home. They were smoking, leaning on the windowsill, they didn't hear me because of the lawnmower outside on the grass. I retreated and listened to them. At one point Amanda called him Costa. Who knows where he comes from, where he's going, with that bulging bag. He brought her some issues of *Internazionale*.

He asked her about the exams she's studying for. What exams, I didn't even go to the classes, my daughter answered.

Rubina stops stirring the mixture with her wooden spoon.

"And you didn't know?"

I knew she was connected remotely. It was just a lie to keep me out of her room.

"What else did they say?" and she opens a bottle of wine.

I escaped like a thief, I'd stolen their confidences. On the stairs I almost ran into that woman from the second floor, on her way out; I didn't even apologize. Outside the smell of cut grass and my car in front of the garage. I left, tires screeching, as if I were stealing that, too.

"Where did you go?" Rubina asks, handing me a glass.

"To my father's."

I turned off the engine next to the Brava. Sometimes this is still my home. He was kneeling in the garden: when his back pain is too intense he works on his knees. With his most sensitive touch he piles the earth around the tomato plants he got at the greenhouse. For a moment I wished for the same care, something like consolation. What's wrong, he asked. She's not studying anymore, I said softly, more to myself than to him. He had figured it out, that it was about Amanda. Your daughter needs a scolding, he said, you're too soft. And what about that other one, what sort of father is he.

He got up effortfully, with one hand on his back, at the most painful point. The tear in one pant leg annoyed him. He doesn't use the knee pads I bought him: if the neighbors saw him he'd be embarrassed, he's not a soccer player. I'm ashamed of other things, I say to Rubina, who listens to me as she sips.

"Today I eavesdropped on Amanda's conversation, the other day I looked at her phone."

"That doesn't seem so serious. If your daughter doesn't speak to you, you almost have to."

It's not only that. At my age I run to my father for comfort. What can he understand about his granddaughter.

"Where are they now?" Rubina asks.

They must have gone out, I didn't see them. But the boy's bag remained where it was, on the couch.

"Afterward bring them the rest of the baccalà, there's a lot."

We set everything out on a small table in the building's

garden. She tends that garden as if it were hers. The cactuses are ready to burst into fleeting and heart-breaking bloom.

The evening is warm, dense with perfumes. The windows in my apartment are dark.

"I'm sorry if I keep talking about her. How's your son?" I ask.

Rubina finishes chewing, swallows.

"Fine, according to him. He never leaves work."

He calls her every Sunday at the same time; sometimes they're looking for him at the job and he has to break off. He likes baccalà so much, if he were sitting with us he'd have at least seconds.

"In London he surely won't find it the way you cook it."

"They say that in London you find everything, but I don't believe it."

"They" are her son and his English wife. Rubina saw them for a week at Christmas and one in the summer, when people were still free to travel. She counts the time that's passed since the last visit, a slight sadness in her voice. They'll come in July.

"They make a stop with me and then go on to their real vacation, in Salento. They're right, it's boring for them here after a while."

For her, especially. She's nice, even affectionate, but she can't really find anything to interest her. And in the end even Giulio doesn't know how to spend the days. His few remaining friends have become almost strangers. He meets them on the avenue, pinches their children's cheeks. They no longer have anything to say to one another.

"Here at home it's burdensome, too: he uses English with his wife and Italian with me—he's translating continuously."

"Aren't you taking lessons on Thursdays?"

"I'm trying, but I'm hardly going to learn at sixty. English is unfriendly to me."

She should go to London more often, I tell her. She's been only twice, she confesses. Already on the plane she felt like an illiterate, she couldn't understand the flight attendant. She visited the main monuments and museums, she heard the choir at Westminster Abbey.

"The city is more tiring than the mountain paths. It's a different tiredness, empty."

She adds something I don't follow, distracted by the darkness on the third floor.

"Maybe I'm losing my daughter," I think aloud.

Rubina reflects for a moment, pours me a little more wine.

"Children—there are so many ways of losing them. It's inevitable at a certain point," she says.

"But mine is ill and I still don't know what's wrong with her, I don't know how to help her."

"Later is when you'll really lose her, when she has the strength to go." She rolls the stem of the glass between her fingers, in one direction, then the other. "How many more days of my life will I spend with my son? Giulio's bought a house in London."

I look at her in surprise: she hadn't told me anything about that.

11.

It seemed an ordinary evening in August, the year I was twenty. I was lounging around the house, irritated by the heat. My mother answered the phone, her face changed in an instant. It's Osvaldo, she said, handing the receiver to my father. I moved closer, something had happened. I couldn't make out the words, but I could hear the agitation in his voice.

"You're sure she isn't anywhere?" he asked.

Then he spoke only in monosyllables, yes and no. He listened attentively.

"All right, I'll bring her," he said finally, looking at me.

He hung up the phone and sighed.

"Put on your shoes and take a sweater. We have to go up to Dente del Lupo."

He asked my mother to find the flashlight. She didn't want me to go but was silent. We heard him rummaging around in the other room. He came out with the cartridge belt in one hand and the gun in the other, he hadn't even put it in the case.

He hurried down the stairs, my mother and I behind.

"Don't go into the woods with them, stay with Nunziatina," she said to me softly.

She was the only one who called the Sheriff by her real name. Osvaldo's wife, the mother of Doralice, who hadn't been seen since that afternoon.

My father put the gun and the flashlight on the rear shelf of the Ritmo we had then, threw the cartridge belt on the seat. He left, accelerating abruptly, and started on the questions.

"You don't know where your friend went?"

I didn't know, no. Behind us the double-barreled gun bounced with every pothole, the flashlight rolled this way and that on the curves. And he, stubborn: "But didn't you say yesterday you were going out together today?"

Yes, but then we'd changed our minds. I'd changed my mind. I'd taken the bus and gone to the beach; some girls who were studying physiotherapy with me were waiting for me in Pescara. I hadn't asked Doralice, they didn't even know one another.

"And what did she do?"

I thought she'd stayed at the campground to help her parents, I said. His questions exasperated me, like the weapon jolted by the potholes, the rolling flashlight.

I had never gone to the mountains with him at night. It was almost nine. On the tree-lined stretches the branches converged overhead as if to crush us, and we barely emerged in time.

He stopped to let some cows cross, a sleepy calf rubbed its mother with its nose. They should have been asleep at that hour, maybe something had disturbed them, maybe the wind.

"Why did you bring the gun?"

He ground his teeth with that spine-chilling sound.

"In certain situations it's better to have it on hand."

"But what situations, what did Osvaldo tell you?"

Nothing specific, only that no one had seen his daughter. When darkness fell, they were alarmed.

"At least it's not loaded?" I asked, pointing behind us.

He nodded.

My father parked near the Sheriff's cabin, in front of the other cars. He slung the gun over his shoulder and hung the cartridge belt at his waist, as if he were going hunting.

She was sitting by herself at a table in the field that was all lit up, like a customer lingering after eating *arrosticini*. Some hair that had escaped the bun was pasted to her sweaty forehead, she was holding her face in her hands. She revived when I approached. She asked me almost the same questions as my father, with some variation.

"Is there a boy involved?"

"I don't think so," I answered.

Then an idea, sudden. She might have gone with someone to the town fair.

"No, she would have said so and, besides, she would have changed. Her skirt and nice shirt are in there," and the Sheriff pointed toward the campground, where the reception office was.

She withdrew into her wait, I hadn't been useful to her. I had never seen her so fragile. She was holding her head so as not to crumple onto the wooden boards of the table.

"If nothing's happened to her, I'll beat her to death myself," she said, but more to herself.

Around Osvaldo the group of hunters, equipped like my father, divided up the areas to cover. But I don't think she's in the woods, said l'Acciarino, why would she go there? Maybe she went with some tourists who were camping here, and they got lost, said a man with a mustache. Is everyone back at the campground? Osvaldo didn't know, by the end of August almost no one was left, and at night those few went to the fairs in the towns. Anyway, they had to search the beechwood, maybe she'd gone for a walk and fallen. But did they need all those guns? They had to carry them of necessity, because of the animals, wild boar and wolves wandering in search of food. Maybe someone was also thinking the worst, but didn't name it. Other voices were mere whispers.

They left in pairs, in different directions. My mother had told me to stay with Nunziatina, but the Sheriff had no intention of sitting there while her daughter was lost. She borrowed a gun and she, too, left. She didn't have a license, but she knew how to shoot.

"Get in the car and go to sleep," and my father handed me the keys.

I stayed in the field for a while, instead. Doralice's grandfather was dozing on a chair. He had returned from the war on foot, in 1945. I looked at that ancient face, burned by the sun, worked by wrinkles. If Doralice had showed up she would have found him and me waiting for her.

The voices and footsteps of the hunters grew distant as they spread out, I could hear rustling, leaves swishing, the predator leaping on the smaller prey, one by one the songs of the night birds. I heard everything. I was afraid of everything. I imagined Doralice hearing every sound amplified, nearby noises, breathing. She, too, was afraid, much more afraid, lost in the dark, with a twisted ankle in a dip in the forest floor. It was my fault, I'd chosen the girls at the beach rather than her. She had proposed a last hike before the bad weather arrived. She'd gone by herself.

I got in the Ritmo, in the faint moonlight. An owl flew toward me from the edge of the beechwood, its broad wings open and spectral. It seemed to want to crash white against the glass, but at the last moment it rose. On the dark side of the mountain points of light were wandering in search of Doralice. It was the flashlights of the hunters and the Sheriff. Through the crack in the window their calls entered: Dorali', Dorali'.

12.

The child comes toward me and I back up very slowly on the rubber mat. With her foot splaying out to the side she aims at the yellow footprints printed on the blue. I encourage her with my voice, my hands, my gaze. A few more steps and she'll finish the course. The doorbell takes her by surprise, she jerks and almost loses her balance. I hold her lightly by one arm, up to the last step. Now she can sit down and rest, and I open the door.

The messenger has a delivery for my daughter. He already tried at home, but no one was there. He comes from Pescara, started his round early this morning. He doesn't know that Amanda and her guest are still sleeping, they got home late last night. It annoyed me to find him on the sofabed this morning; I'm no longer used to the presence of a man. He was uncovered, his boxers with the Vespa printed on the front swelled by a morning erection.

Luckily, the messenger says, he recalled that he could find me at the office. I merely glance at the label, Zalando, and the invitation "Love me. Wear me." I put the child's socks and shoes on, her mother is on the stairs. Her muscle tone is improving, I reassure her. We'll see each other next week, I say, caressing her hair, held in place by a gold hairband.

Amanda hasn't received anything since she returned. I pick up the box and it almost flies out of my hands—I was expecting it to be heavier. I tip it in one direction, then the other, inside is a rustling that shifts. If I turn it upside down something hard, perhaps metallic, hits the packing. It's not those sweat clothes she wears, I hear a thin fabric, maybe cotton or viscose. The label doesn't help: order number, bar code. I imagine a dress with a belt and a buckle, that's what's knocking against the sides of the box.

In the last years of high school, Amanda wore minimal outfits, cut low in the back. She celebrated all the birthdays, even of kids older than she was.

I didn't oppose it. She was a teenager who gave me no worries. She didn't smoke, or come home drunk, no gaudy piercings or tattoos appeared on her body. Other mothers described their children's excesses, the years of school lost. I listened to them with a sense of distance. I was lucky, with Amanda.

Some Saturdays I'd drive her to one of the clubs on the coast. She wanted me to drop her off a little way from the entrance. Her father would take care of her return, so late at night.

After her graduation we went away for a week. She chose Barcelona. She never tired of wandering through the Parc Güell: she touched the colored mosaics, admired Gaudí's salamander with a child's sense of wonder. For the first time my husband didn't come on vacation with us.

I shake the package and don't know on what occasion Amanda will wear the dress I hear. She hasn't gone out since the day of our walk in the mountains. She wears pajamas or sweat clothes, the T-shirt with the café logo if she's going to work. But now they need her only on weekends. She serves customers without ever looking them in the face, so the owners prefer to have her washing cups and glasses. That's what Rubina reported, she knows the owners. I never go to that café.

Milan gave me back a depleted daughter. The box I'm turning over in my hands might contain a hope. Someone here will have remembered her, invited her to a party. Amanda answered, decided to go, will wear the dress she ordered on Zalando. She'll take out her favorite sandals from the life of before, the ones whose top strap looks like a snake. It will be a new beginning. It's June, a summer without limits is starting. In time the desire to study will return, too, maybe closer to home.

I try to remove the tape. I stop, Amanda will know if I've opened her package. I put it down on the desk, I see her against the light, dancing as when she was eighteen. It's only yesterday, but everything's different.

Or maybe she's already regretted the purchase. She'll throw the dress on the chair in her room, without even trying it. If it's black I could wear it myself to the first choir concert. It will be outside, at the sea, Maestro Milo's been offered the Flaiano Auditorium, in Pescara.

I left her too much alone in the city. When she returned she was someone else. I thought she was absorbed by new friendships; they existed only in my imagination.

After she'd gone I filled the days with patients. I sought exhaustion in work. At home Amanda's empty room was added to the cold half of the double bed. They had left a few months apart, father and daughter. My husband, our daughter. In November I turned off the radiator and closed the door in the room where she'd grown up. I confronted winter.

She has to be free, I said to myself, that's why I didn't get on a train. Feeling weak inside, I confined myself to daily gestures, I didn't dare more. I didn't want her to see me as I was. I tamed the fear I had for her at first. A place she'd so longed for couldn't hurt her.

Before grabbing her purse, they hit her hard on the ear. She didn't even see them, the street was dark right there. They came up quietly from behind, she only had the impression that there were three, tall and thin. Her head was spinning and a very sharp whistle deafened her. She leaned against an SUV parked along the sidewalk and slid to the ground. Later, calling from an unknown number, she couldn't tell me how long she'd sat there, crying, in the dust. Blood dripped from her earlobe, her earring had wounded her.

She couldn't tell me if anyone had passed by, certainly no one helped her. It happened one night, in the seven minutes it took to walk from the metro stop to her house.

The roommate who opened the door listened to her for a moment, both standing in the doorway. She didn't see the blood on her ear, on the collar of the jacket. She lent her the phone to call me and apologized, she had an exam the next day.

"She didn't even offer me a glass of water," Amanda said.

I consoled her as well as I could, from a distance. That time I really was wrong not to get on the train. Respecting her freedom, I failed her when she needed me. Some boundaries are too subtle for an indecisive mother like me. But do the most stable parents know at every moment the truth of what to do?

"Don't worry, it will pass," and I believed her.

I still have a doubt that she didn't tell me everything about that night. Basically nothing serious had happened to her, I thought then. They had stolen only her prepaid card and the phone. The wound was superficial, it would soon heal. I didn't see the more lasting damage, the trust in the world that had been ripped away from her, along with the purse.

She soon forgot the episode, so it seemed. She didn't want to talk about it with me or with her father. She still has a reflex that makes her jump at sudden contact. At night she sleeps with the light on and when dawn comes in through the window Amanda turns it off and gives in to a deeper sleep. I find it touching that she sometimes carries in her pocket a useless pocketknife.

13.

The summer I got married Doralice came back from Canada for a few weeks. By the time I found out it was late, I had long since sent the invitations. My other friends would all come. It was just a few days before when I sent her the invitation, to her parents' address. The favor of a response is kindly requested, it said. No word from her, not even a phone call to congratulate me. Maybe she had already left, maybe I should have called her or, better still, asked her in person. But I was so busy then.

We ran into each other in front of the hairdresser's. I was trying out a style and emerged with my hair gathered in a chignon. Doralice was carrying shopping bags from the supermarket. We stopped in the sun. So you're getting married, she said, her accent slightly altered by English. Yes, we decided in the spring, Dario and I.

"It's time, don't you think? I'm twenty-eight."

I immediately regretted that. She was the same age, with no plans for a family, or she didn't say anything. She seemed alone. But really what did I know of her life there, except that she lived in Toronto. I couldn't imagine her in the skyscrapers on the lake, in the six-months-long winter. Who had Doralice become?

Meanwhile she was sweating, in ill-fitting jeans, a synthetic T-shirt. I was also hot, I touched her arm to lead her into the shade of a cornice. She put the shopping down on the sidewalk, I saw what she had bought for her mother: detergent, boxes of pasta.

"Will you come?" I asked.

She looked at me for a moment, then bent over to shift a bag. She hadn't brought a nice dress, she said, straightening. "And my flight is the next day, I have to get ready," she added.

I sighed, even I don't know if it was disappointment or relief. A lock of hair fell on my neck.

"Don't worry about the dress, the ceremony's informal," I reassured her. "You can come at the last minute, if you change your mind."

She would think about it, but it was difficult. I shouldn't count her for the restaurant. And then: "I won't keep you, you must have such a lot to do."

She said goodbye with an effort to smile. She picked up her bags and went off into the sun, without turning. She had forgotten to wish me well.

I didn't think of her again in those days. I went to dinner with Dario to taste all the dishes for the wedding lunch, and the wines. I laughed, drunk and happy. We chose the names of the children we would have. Amanda, for a girl. In our imaginations she was born that night.

It took ten minutes for the mayor to join us in matrimony. He read the obligations of the spouses and pointed out where to sign.

"That's a wedding?" my father asked his fellow in-law, not exactly in a whisper.

Doralice didn't come, the friends we had been no longer existed. The joy of that day was scarcely touched by it.

At the restaurant my mother handed me a white envelope, Osvaldo had brought it the night before. Give it to Lucia tomorrow, he had said. I glanced inside: a hundred-euro note and a card from all the family. Surely Nunziatina had asked Doralice to write it in beautiful calligraphy. That was how I received her congratulations, round and regular.

An enlarged photo from that day hangs on the wall behind

the television in my father's house. In the middle us newlyweds, on either side my parents in their wedding outfits. She was resigned to all that was lacking: the train, the church decorated with flowers, the priest's words that would make her cry. He was a little stiff, the pleated collar of my dress in contrast with his blue one.

I have no idea how much it bothers him now to see Dario in front of him. If he doesn't take down the picture it's only out of devotion to my mother, who put it under glass and hung it there. But I look at it every time I go. On that wall I'm still married. For my whole life, I'm sure of it, as I clutch the bouquet. I smile at the hazy yet radiant future to come.

Dario and I: I struggle to understand where we faltered years later. In habit, in silences, between bodies increasingly distant in the bed. I answer every question with another, in a chain that I can't end.

I've used up the courage of that bride, the dreams. I'm no longer her age, I don't have her strength. Some mornings I'd refuse to get up, like Amanda. I'd like to sink into a free and irresponsible sleep for a day, a week, or more. Serve only myself, forget the others. My father asks me to come with him on the last stretch of his journey, insisting that I take that land. I have to restore the world to my daughter. They pull me in their own direction, to their own need. They're breaking me.

14.

Osvaldo waits for me at the landslide that blocks the road to his house. He invites me to park in a space where I'll find the car later in the shade of the acacias. The mass of earth that flowed down off the hill is now dry and cracked, infested by low plants. It's been like that for years, the work of removal would cost the town too much.

"It's not worth it," says Osvaldo, "for the two old people who are still there."

He apologizes for the Ape, covered with a thick dust. Inside it's small and clean, smelling of pine-scented Little Trees. He takes me to the land that belongs to him. I recognize the landscape, the round bales of hay poised on the stubble.

The last time I came it was because of Doralice, that year, when we were still girls.

"I could have spoken to you on the phone, but I thought it would be a pleasure for the Sheriff to see you after so long," says Osvaldo.

He's always called his wife the Sheriff, Nunziatina only on more serious occasions. The idea of the *casotto* and the campground came to her when Dente del Lupo was just a pasture for the shepherds who lived farther down. Like Osvaldo and my father. But then, in the summer, tourists started coming, asking where they could eat *arrosticini* and pecorino. And if they could pitch their tents in the fields.

"This winter she had a bad fall," says Osvaldo.

The Sheriff doesn't want to go to the Thursday market

anymore. She no longer makes bread in the brick oven, he buys it in the town.

Nunziatina's in the farmyard, shouting: Shoo, shoo, and waving her arms. The chicks run here and there. She hasn't heard the Ape, when she sees us we've already gotten out. I go up to her and we're embarrassed for a moment, not knowing how to greet each other. Then she wipes her hands on the apron and takes one of mine, holds it tight. She diffuses an intense heat, the memory of her strength. She points to a white hen standing back, bewildered, head and neck stripped of feathers.

"Someone gave her to Osvaldo the other day, she's a good layer. But the others are jealous, they peck at her."

Hens can be fierce.

When I was a child a rumor circulated about my father and the Sheriff. Someone had seen them going into the woods, she ahead and a little later he, like a dog trailing the odor of the bitch. My mother dismissed the gossip with a wave of her hand and a slightly nervous laugh. I was there, too, when a neighbor reported it to her, we were soaping clothes in the wash house. They didn't name him, but I understood who they were talking about.

My mother preferred not to know his misdeeds, since she couldn't leave him. Where would she go, with me so little? She had nothing except a modest dowry. Her parents wouldn't have wanted us. And then, it was true, people gossiped out of envy. They were a handsome couple.

Not even I know the truth about my father. Once I heard that he visited the whores on the coast, when he happened to be in Pescara. I was already eavesdropping then, on the adults' conversations.

I know he loved my mother until the last day, in his rough way. Until the final hour he cleaned her mouth with a batiste handkerchief that he washed by hand at night. I escaped, everything that comes out of the mouth disturbs me. Words sometimes more than saliva.

And yet I couldn't hate the Sheriff. She was affectionate with me, she saw me grow up along with her daughter. In the farmyard, which has stayed the same, I regret that I never came to see her, after Doralice left. She's old now, I'm middle-aged. There isn't time to recover the good that's been lost.

She invites me into the kitchen on the ground floor. We sit at the table, Osvaldo opens a beer and gulps it down.

"Go easy, you're taking those medicines," she warns him.

She's a little puffy, the capillaries in evidence on her cheeks. She offers me her walnut liqueur.

"I'm tired, I don't feel like doing anything. Anyway, who eats all this stuff?" and she gestures at the pantry. "Let's hope my daughter comes this summer," she murmurs.

For a moment we hear only the slats of the shade on the door, stirred by the air. The hen has come in, crouches on the floor like a cat.

Osvaldo chases her out, sits down at the table with another beer. He has to water the garden, he says. He's worried about the thirsty earth, the fruit that's burned by the sun before it ripens. The potatoes no longer last until the next harvest. The Sheriff interrupts him.

"Let's not waste time with complaints. It's like that everywhere, for her father, too."

Here he is, I was waiting for him. As soon as he's named he takes over the room. Osvaldo sighs.

"From now on your father wants me to talk to you about Dente del Lupo."

"Why? He's always decided everything himself."

"He says he's ill, he won't last much longer."

"What is it you want to tell me about Dente del Lupo?"

Osvaldo takes a roundabout approach, he starts with a man who pastures his cows in that area. Last week he lost a calf, not a small one, almost a heifer. He searched for three days, then he followed a stink of carrion. He went into the old campground, at the point where the fence is ripped. The calf must have gone through there as well, maybe driven by a wolf. It was lying at the bottom of the empty pool, legs broken, eye still frightened. Osvaldo sees I'm stricken, pours some more walnut liqueur into my glass, ignoring my protests. He drains his beer.

"For a breeder a calf is a big loss," he says, repressing a burp. "The man went to protest to the town and the Forest Service."

Osvaldo will have to compensate him, or he'll sue him and my father.

"I built on it, but the land belongs to him."

"To the two of you," the Sheriff corrects him, looking straight at me.

The campground can't remain abandoned, it's dangerous. And what if a person fell into that pool?

"You're the owner now. We have to decide what to do with Dente del Lupo."

15.

So I took it. The dead calf and Osvaldo's fine were more convincing than my father's insistence. In a lifetime he hasn't learned that he gets the opposite when he tries to force me to obey.

Yesterday I made a new appointment with the notary and today we're already leaving his office. Certainly they had talked; Ruzzi hurried our little business, for fear I might change my mind. They've always gone hunting together, though they couldn't be more different.

"He didn't want anything, just the expenses," my father congratulates himself going down the stairs. "But last time I let him get a really fine rabbit."

"He killed it?"

"Of course, that's why you go."

We leave the building, he looks around.

"Let's have a drink, since we're in Pescara," he proposes.

He wants to celebrate the deed. Now Dente del Lupo is mine, he's given it to me. A few signatures was all it took, under the notary's attentive eyes. My father struggled a bit, after each one he went back to dot the i's and cross the t's.

"So you won't pay the inheritance tax, afterward," he said at the end, and Ruzzi nodded.

After all, it wasn't difficult to register those parcels of land in my name. Places can't be guilty. How can Dente del Lupo be guilty of the shots, the blood? It dripped into the under-brush: one of the girls was found with a handkerchief over a wound, but she lacked the strength to press it. No molecule of that blood remains in the earth, at the roots of the vegetation. Some thirty years have passed. Everything has evaporated, transformed, decomposed. Even nature forgets. It overgrows tragedies and disasters.

"Cheers!" says my father, touching my glass with his.

He ordered a hot *ponce* digestif, in this mugginess. It took the waitress a while to find the bottle—who in Pescara would order that, in summer.

Today I received my inheritance, a burden in advance. A bit of the mountain belongs to me. I repeat that silently, in front of him as he blows on the steam. I fell into the trap, finally. His shadow lengthens, bends over me, warm and imperious. He'll still be there, afterward.

"Better the woods than an apartment in the city," he said from his terrace, pointing out the place, when I came to pick him up.

I'll have to protect land and plants, animals and people passing through. How, I don't know. I'll decide with Osvaldo, but he's old, too, he was old before his time. Doralice's the one I should talk to about it.

THE GIRLS

1.

My father tore up the mountain road that night, after Osvaldo's phone call. He barely downshifted on the bends, accelerated to the maximum on the short straightaways. For a moment he opened the window, then closed it because of the cold air. Suddenly he looked at me, his face red.

"You girls will kill us, with your crazy shenanigans."

He gripped the Ritmo's steering wheel, his knuckles white, and shook his head. What did I have to do with it, I hadn't even seen Doralice that day. But we were the same, she and I, always ready for adventure, without thinking of the consequences. I had no idea where she'd got to, and it was completely dark by now.

"The mountain is dangerous at night if you don't know it well. You don't see the gorges, the abysses, if you fall in you won't be found."

Sometimes the woods thinned out, clouds covered the moon and passed by rapidly. There must be a strong wind up there. I didn't answer him. Only his gun, bumping along in the back, the rolling flashlight.

His rage at my last foray with Doralice hadn't yet cooled. We'd taken her uncle's old motorbike out and had ended up off the road near the fishing lake. I still had scratches on my arms from the thorns. We just wanted to be young.

Sleep in the car, my father said before going off with the others in search of Doralice. From the passenger seat I observed her grandfather, in the circle of light from the *casotto* so still on the chair that sometimes I doubted he was alive. I was alone. I knew already that I would stay awake. If something happened to me he wouldn't notice: deaf, his eyes closed. I was ashamed of that thought, safe inside the Ritmo while my friend had disappeared.

Maybe she was only getting home late from a party, and the Sheriff, coming down from the mountain, would give her a beating in front of everyone. Then I remembered the kidnappings in Sardinia and Calabria, the kidnapped in dens in the middle of the woods. Neither Osvaldo nor my father would ever have been able to pay a ransom.

A snap behind the car, followed by a thud. I waited without breathing, a mad hammer in my chest. Some of the shepherds swore that bears had returned to our area, at least two adult specimens. Or maybe the same one, spied in different places. I heard nothing else. I had to calm down. It was the wind gusting through the beechwood, breaking branches. It was that nervous moon, covered and uncovered by clouds.

I was trembling with cold. My father had told me he'd thrown an old jacket in the trunk. I resisted for a long time before making up my mind. The wind tugged the door as soon as I opened it, around me movements, noises in the dark. In an instant I opened the trunk, grabbed one sleeve, and got back inside. I covered myself from neck to legs, the jacket smelled of sheep and earth. In a pocket one of my father's knives. I held it tight and must have fallen asleep.

Approaching headlights woke me. The moon had shifted slightly, the peak of Dente del Lupo pierced it. The car stopped on the other side of the road, in front of a Renault 4. A man and a woman headed for the gate of the campground, carrying sleeping children, legs dangling. They didn't see me. Only then I noticed the red Renault.

Later I heard shots, two sharp pops repeated by the echo. I started, and the jacket slid to my feet. They were far away, in the direction of the pass. Maybe it had been my father. At least something was happening, soon I would know about Doralice.

More time passed, and a small light began moving along the ridge. Sometimes I lost it, then it reappeared lower down, a little closer. Others could be seen where the beechwood thinned out. They were descending toward the *casotto*. I waited for them in the field; the wind had fallen. The grandfather, skin and bones on the chair, was stone.

The Sheriff was the first to come out of the woods, she threw down the flashlight, still lighted.

"We didn't find her," she said.

Her voice was worn out, as if she'd been shouting for all those hours. She asked me nothing, she understood that there was no news here. The others arrived, two at a time. The shots were an agreed-on signal to come down from the mountain.

They set the guns on a table and gathered, standing. With a glance my father assured himself that I was all right.

"Osva', you have to make a report to the police," he said, taking him by the arm.

The Sheriff moaned, sat down in front of all those guns. She said that was true, it had to be done. With a nod she summoned her husband, who was still staring into space. She pointed to the road: go, I'll wait here.

"We'll take you to the station," my father offered.

We got in silently, me in the back. He turned the car, grinding in reverse. The headlights illuminated the license plate of the Renault: MO 250645, and that thought came to Osvaldo. Stop a moment, he said. He left the door open and ran to the campsite. My father turned to look at me, as if I knew why.

Osvaldo returned immediately, hands at his temples.

"The girls from Modena are missing, too. They're not in their tent."

2.

Every so often I heard them talking, a few idle phrases. We descended, rounding bend after bend; sometimes I fell into a half sleep. With the headlights my father greeted a shepherd in a three-wheel truck, milk cans in the back.

"It's Ciarango going up to the pen," he said.

In the town we saw no one, Osvaldo rang the bell, and after a while the door of the police station opened. I leaned on the window, waiting.

"Get in front."

I couldn't bear it when my father used his tone of command, but at the moment I could only obey him.

"You have to tell me the truth. Even if it's ugly, nothing will happen to you."

"But what do you want from me? You, the Sheriff. I don't know where Doralice went."

That wasn't possible, for him. We were friends, we spent hours on the phone. He spoke into my face, with that spoiled night breath.

"I'm not her bodyguard. Leave me alone."

He remained silent only for a moment.

"Did she run away with someone?"

"No. I don't know."

He seized me roughly by the chin, forced my head toward him.

"Look at me when you answer. Be careful, I'll know if you're lying."

I pushed his hand back, he calmed down. I could say that: after all, there'd be nothing bad about it. My aunt had run away with her boyfriend and later they got married. Even if I was a child at the time, I remembered it: my father had gone out with his gun to kill them both. I had been afraid for them, that night, and for him, who would become a murderer.

"Times have changed," I told him. "We don't need to run away with our boyfriends."

"And the girls from the north? Might she have gone with them?"

He had seen the Renault 4 on the side of the road. How had they left, on foot?

"Eh, with you girls one never knows. You think I didn't find out when you and Doralice went hitchhiking?"

"Every so often we make a move, we're not always at home working on our embroidery."

Just then Osvaldo appeared in the doorway of the station, his gaze dark. He came toward the Ritmo, I got out to give him the seat, relieved. He stopped on my father's side, instead, and said the police wanted to talk to me.

So we all sat down with the grizzled marshal, me in the middle. He observed me for a while, before starting. "Signorina, you can help us find your friend."

He offered me a cup of water, I didn't want it. He had a warm, deep voice, the accent of somewhere in the south. On the table a framed group photo, maybe his family. The tears I had been holding back since evening were suddenly released. I shouldn't worry, he reassured me, it wasn't an interrogation. He just wanted some information. But I was weeping for Doralice: in the presence of that red and black uniform, under the flickering neon, I lost her. My father found a crumpled dirty handkerchief in his pocket; I preferred to dry my face with my hands. I composed myself.

"Did Doralice tell you what she was going to do yesterday?"

Crying had weakened me. I thought she had stayed at the campground, I said. I was silent about not having invited her to the beach. With my friends from Pescara I would be ashamed of how she spoke, of her strong mountain accent, the dialect words that every so often escaped her. And the way she waved her arms wildly in the water, like a person who doesn't know how to swim but pretends to.

At that moment a younger sergeant arrived, with sculpted sideburns. He remained standing, listening.

The usual questions about boyfriends, Doralice didn't have one, but sometimes she went out with someone. He worked at Riccione in the summer and didn't know anything, the Sheriff had called him.

But did she meet someone up at the *casotto*?

I wasn't aware of it. I was sweating as I faced the two policemen, between my father and Osvaldo.

"What can you tell me about the girls from Modena? Do you know them?" the marshal continued.

Not well, we'd gone out together once.

"By yourselves?"

"No, in a group."

Osvaldo said he'd seen them that morning, at the campground. But his daughter wasn't with them.

"They were wearing short shorts and hiking boots, but I don't know if they meant to go climbing in the mountains."

The sergeant interrupted: "These tourists, they go around with bare thighs and then there's trouble."

"What are you talking about? Keep your comments to yourself," the marshal reprimanded him.

"And if my daughter doesn't come back?" Osvaldo asked, twisting his hands.

"Let's wait a few hours, it might be only a girl's prank."

Maybe he had finished with me. Instead he stared at me again, he didn't believe me.

"And the man who brings the beverages up to the *casotto*, do you know him?"

No, I lied. I knew only that he came from another town.

"But Doralice knows him."

It wasn't a question. I turned toward Osvaldo, but he was looking the other way.

"She did, yes, she had to," I said.

Where did the man with the drinks come from?

"From Isola."

3.

Then I went to the men's bathroom, where I cried again. On the mirror dried sprays of water and, above, my changed face. A late-summer night carried me abruptly to adulthood. There was nothing safe out there, there was no Doralice. With every minute I felt she was more dead. And what I was going through I would never forget.

At a certain point life accelerates. Afterward everything remains fixed in an image or a sound of the moment. One always returns to it. I could say this to Amanda, if I could find the words. She asked me again about those girls.

There was no toilet paper, the soap was a yellowish chip. The dryer had a defective sound. I dried my hands on the front of my shirt, sour with sweat.

The policemen got ready, Marshal Capasso on the phone. My father and Osvaldo were already outside, next to the car, talking. They gave me a suspicious look when I approached.

"Did she go out with that fellow? He's at least ten years older than you."

"We're adults, Osvaldo, we go out with whoever we want."

My father punched the window of the Ritmo.

"Tonight I'll kill you in front of the police station," he threatened between his teeth.

Shortly afterward two policemen rang the bell of a small house in the new neighborhood of Isola. A sleepy woman opened the door, in alarm. Her husband was sleeping, she said, he'd come home late from the deliveries.

They entered without asking permission. They called him by name and surname, asked him point blank where he'd been the day before. He was still lying down and understood nothing. He sat up on the bed and began to recall his movements, but they were impatient. Had he gone to Dente del Lupo, yes or no? To unload beer at the *casotto*, as usual. The Sheriff had signed the receipt. And then? Then he had continued his round. Had he seen her daughter? Had she by any chance got in the truck with him?

His wife had put a bathrobe on over her summer pajamas; leaning against the doorpost she looked at him, biting her lip. She listened to him swear that between him and the girl who had disappeared there was nothing. One of the two cops wanted the keys and glanced around the van outside. He shifted some cases of Coca-Cola.

The next morning at the market in Isola people were already talking about that man who'd just got married and was screwing the Sheriff's daughter. They did it in the woods, and he even brought her home when his wife was at work. In the gossip of those hours the version I knew from Doralice herself swelled into an affair that lasted for months. Instead it had been a quickie on the seat of the van. Maybe someone had seen them behind the *casotto*, where he piled up the cases and took back the empties to turn in. Or maybe he boasted about it in the bar in the town: he'd been with a twenty-year-old.

It seemed to me I recognized him one night a while ago, on the waterfront road in Pescara. His head, white by now, on the body of that time, only a little less muscular. I didn't trust my memory, I didn't greet him. He looked at me for a moment as well and then kept going.

That night I returned to Dente del Lupo with Osvaldo and my father. The Renault 4 was still there. The Sheriff had moved to the campground, to a kind of office. She kept an eye on the phone, and every so often picked up the receiver to be sure it was working. I thought of calling my mother, certainly awake and worried. I wanted to tell her I was fine, and Doralice hadn't been found. Maybe it wasn't the right thing, in front of the Sheriff. She wouldn't have let me occupy the line even for a minute anyway. Her husband asked if she had the documents of the girls from Modena.

"Why?"

"The police need them. If the girls aren't back in a few hours they have to inform the family."

She stared at him, looking for meaning in his words. She began to rummage in a drawer, at first furiously, then wearily. She found an ID card, gave it to them.

"There's this, the other has only her license and she took it with her."

"You look, you can see better," and Osvaldo handed it to me.

I opened it, to the faint smile of Tania Vignati, height 1.68 meters, resident of Bomporto (MO). When we went out together, a few nights earlier, she had said they preferred to pass themselves off as Modenese, no one had heard of their town. You think anyone's heard of ours, Doralice had responded, laughing, over the Campari. In the ID photo her eyes were vivid in her face: natural, without makeup. That night at the bar, on the other hand, she and her sister had the same lipstick and eyelashes thick with mascara.

"Yes, she's the younger one, the one who's twenty," and I gave the document back to Osvaldo.

The Sheriff barely looked at him. Framed on the wall behind her was the Madonna of the Seven Swords, one for each of her sufferings.

I went out in search of air. The pool at the campground was a black rectangle at the far end, beyond the glow of the lights. When it was built people came just to see it, a real pool in this area. In a few steps I came to the first tent sites, all empty. Sometimes by the end of August it was already fall up there. Osvaldo kept the sites clear of grass and rocks, so that they wouldn't be lumpy under the backs of sleeping campers. Otherwise he left daisies and mullein free to flower. Here was the place where, when Doralice and I were kids, we had put up a tent. I don't remember who had lent it to us, it must have been the summer her parents opened the campground. We played at being tourists, but we weren't prepared, and a single night of sleeping between old blankets was enough for us. In the morning we were awakened by the sheep grazing nearby, the enclosure wasn't ready yet.

It hadn't been possible to fence it off on the woods side, then or later. The two sisters had camped there, in the shelter of a beech. Osvaldo had advised against it, because of the wild animals. But they weren't afraid, in fact were looking for them.

I could barely glimpse their tent, it was almost dark at that point. I approached, slowly unzipped the flap. I touched something soft like a body, but without heat. Then, by feel, I found a flashlight and turned it on. It was only a bulging backpack, beside a large, full purse. The sleeping bags were empty, on one of them a big book. I recalled what they had said that night at the bar: vacation is about to end, they'd be leaving Saturday morning. I discovered that they were already preparing to go. And Saturday had barely begun.

4.

He found her around two, near Pietra Rotonda. There was something out of place between light and dark. He aimed the flashlight straight on: scratched legs, earth-stained. He illuminated her entirely. The head was turned in the other direction, toward the cliff. Hey, hear me? he said. He bent over and pressed his fingers against her neck. No pulse, the skin cold, rigid. He went to the other side to get a better look at the face, and recognized her. He stood for a moment beside her, seconds or minutes. He couldn't say later, at the trial.

From the window that night I saw the light running toward us. He had crossed the ravines of the Inferno, to shorten the distance. Someone's coming, I said.

Marshal Capasso had transformed the Sheriff's office into a kind of headquarters. He followed by radio the men on the Mountain Rescue team who were searching. Every so often he looked at her, his consoling phrases useless.

I remember the young man from the Italian Alpine Club at the door, out of breath. Sweat dripped from his reddish hair. Behind him Osvaldo, with those eyes. He already knew, he'd been out there with my father. The Sheriff stood up suddenly. She knew Dario, a look was enough for her. I also knew him, even though we had never gone out together. He was three years older, muscles molded by trekking, and a smile showing strong teeth, which still moves me when I leaf through our photos. We wouldn't have believed at the time that a night so black would bind us.

In front of him the Sheriff crumpled onto the chair and nearly fell on the floor. For a few moments she lost consciousness, Osvaldo slapped her awake. It's not Doralice, it's not Doralice, he repeated gently.

"Give the young man some water," the marshal said, and started with the questions. Who had he found?

Dario drank and then: one of the two sisters, he answered, he had seen them in the town but didn't know their names. The one with the short hair and a blond streak on one side.

Capasso unfolded the ID card, Dario looked at the photo. A nod, and a sob escaped. Tania Vignati was the girl in the woods.

I slid down the wall and sat on the floor. I hugged my legs to keep hold of a sudden stomach ache. Dario remained standing, he was in a hurry to lead them to Pietra Rotonda. He was sweaty and panting.

"You're sure she's dead?"

"Marshal, I've done the course. I can recognize the living from the dead."

But it was the first time he'd seen it, he said, bursting into tears.

"Does she have blood on her, wounds?"

Blood on the shirt, which was torn a little. He dried his face with the back of his hand. Could you see animal bites? He didn't think so, but he hadn't examined her that closely. He had seen some traces, yes, in the mud not far away.

"Wolves?"

Maybe, also, but it was confusing.

"And then hoofprints from a shod horse."

"Horses don't kill," the marshal said.

Nor do wolves, as a matter of fact. And yet the *Corriere Abruzzese* the next morning was headlined *Three Modenese Girls Missing*, while the article criticized the repopulation of wolves.

"Where is it precisely?"

"Near the wall we use for climbing."

"We have to search the area. Living or dead, the others won't be far."

That phrase escaped the marshal, but the Sheriff didn't even hear it, she was elsewhere. She, too, wondered if her daughter's heart was still beating, or not.

"The shepherds know that area inch by inch," said Osvaldo.

"But they don't say much, I don't know that they'll be any help," Capasso answered.

Then he called the police in Bomporto. They had to warn the Vignati family. For the moment only that the daughters had disappeared from the campground. He read the address given on the ID card.

I pulled a chair over to the Sheriff and leaned against her warmth. I didn't expect that arm around my shoulders. At some point she hugged me. She was trembling, and I with her. Just then I wasn't thinking of Doralice. I was thinking of Tania, who was our age. A few nights before in the bar she'd been wearing a flowered dress, a jade necklace hanging on her breast. For years I saw her like that in my sleepless nights, laughing and drinking with us, forever a girl, with the necklace that shifted with her breathing. I remember the shadings of green in the beads. She was worried about her biology exam, in early September. She said she couldn't study at the campground. And lucky us who lived here: where they lived, on the plain, the mosquitoes devoured you. She was so alive.

5

I'm coming with you, I told them. Osvaldo and my father were going to call Ciarango up at the pen. Along the rocky dirt road they talked about the footprints the boy from the Alpine Club had seen.

"If the horse was shod it has an owner."

Ciarango drove the sheep up to Pietra Rotonda on horseback, maybe he knew something. When we arrived, the big white dogs wanted to eat up the car, Osvaldo's voice soothed them. The shelter was just below the mountaintop. My father knocked with his fists.

It took the shepherd a while to crack open the door. He was holding a flashlight. He recognized the two men immediately, then he aimed it at my face.

"It's my daughter, you don't remember her?"

"What'd you bring her for?" he asked, moving his mouth within his hermit's beard.

He lowered the light to see the rest of me. He let us enter the single room and sat on his cot.

"Get the wine," he said to me.

He lit up the table, which was loaded with dirty plates, cans of beans, wine bottles, most of them empty. A half cheese had been dug out with a knife. I didn't move.

He had a house and family down below, but in summer he forgot about them. The other shepherds said he was rich, but where he kept the money was anyone's guess. He was also a pensioner, by now.

"We didn't come to drink," my father said. "They found a girl dead at Pietra Rotonda, do you know anything?"

He shook his head no, without surprise. Lambs died, girls died, to him it didn't make much difference.

"But there were hoofprints from your horse in the mud."

Ciarango shrugged. So? They could be from anytime. He didn't keep him in the pen anymore.

"Two other people have disappeared. You know the area, you have to help us," my father said.

"Eh, the tourists get lost. Later they come back."

He blinded us in turn with the flashlight. He didn't want to come with us, he had to milk at dawn.

"But don't you have that foreigner who helps you out?"

"The worker's not here now."

Osvaldo entered the illuminated space.

"One is my daughter," he said.

Then Ciarango got up from his cot, opened his eyes wide. "Who, Doralicia?"

"Doralice."

Some summer nights I was at the *casotto*, too, when he came down on horseback. Ciarango gave me the creeps. The way he stank, his life alone, without a bathroom and without electricity. He was like an animal himself.

Here's the cowboy, Doralice would say, and we'd get the giggles. Stop it, Osvaldo reproached us, you don't understand anything. Gossip. Ciarango dismounted and took a cold beer. His pants so dirty they were stiff. He looked at us suspiciously while we said mean things about him. His horse waited, tied to a beech, at the edge of the field.

"All right, I'll come with the three-wheel truck," he said that night.

He took his time. He looked for his shoes with the light, the knife where he'd stuck it. We went ahead, in first and second gear down along the unpaved road. In his seat Osvaldo was in a frenzy.

"No need to worry about Ciarango," my father reassured him. "He goes his own way, but he wouldn't even kill an ant."

The sergeant was on the road between the *casotto* and the campground, he came over to the car. What happened, Osvaldo asked him.

"It seems they've found something else at Pietra Rotonda."

"Officer, if it's my daughter you'd better tell me."

His voice turning shrill. But nothing certain was known, the marshal was there with other cops and that boy, Dario.

My father and Osvaldo looked at each other only for a moment, they could see also in the dark, like nocturnal birds. A nod toward the campground, where the Sheriff was consumed with anguish.

"Don't say anything to my wife for now."

The two set out, not even noticing that I was behind them. The path was easy for a short stretch, then we entered the woods. Small fragments of starry sky between the foliage of the beeches and the black earth. Osvaldo walked in front, with the flashlight on and a quick step. I stumbled on roots and rocks.

Doralice had asked if I was going to the beach and I had said no. She could have been there soaking with me and the others. At the beach nothing would have happened to her. It seemed to me so long ago and it was yesterday. My skin was still burning from the sun. I wanted her alive, with all of myself. I would have apologized. Once the fear was gone, we'd have fun together again. She would tell me exactly what had happened with the man who brought the drinks. I tripped on a broken branch, held on to my father's back.

When we got to the soft ground he stopped for a moment, looked all around with the light. There they were, the horse's hoofprints in the mud.

"These are fresh," he said, touching one with his finger. "It's strange that Ciarango doesn't know anything."

Another ascent that left you breathless. Osvaldo waited for us at the top. In the other direction the woods opened up suddenly. In the moonlight Pietra Rotonda appeared.

6.

We saw them from above: four or five men were shining light on something. The one squatting must be the marshal, he was pointing to the cliff. Over there, over there, someone shouted. Osvaldo started running down the slope, but I slowed my pace. My legs were weak, I didn't want to get there, I didn't want to know. My father turned, he heard the silence behind him. I followed.

I stopped again, next to the small pack that had fallen on the mushrooms. I was close now, the men gathered around hid her from view. An officer spoke loudly into a radio full of static and interference, he explained the position. A few more steps, and Dario moved. She was so white, she seemed of wax. She had her shirt on, pulled up to the neck, then she was naked down to the socks folded over the hiking boots. A line of ants walked between her breasts, crossed her face on a diagonal, got lost in her hair. Some drifted off into her mouth. I could think only of her arm, lying on a clump of butcher's-broom. I would have liked to take her hand and, even now, move it away from the thorns. My father made the sign of the cross, Osvaldo lowered his head. Then he took off his jacket and, leaning over, was about to cover her pelvis.

"You can't, Osvaldo, we're waiting for the public prosecutor." Capasso stopped him, and he put the light, fluttering jacket back on.

"Marshal, the shorts and underpants are over there," a cop reported.

I closed my eyes and the voices were extinguished, along with the buzzing of the radio, the faint wind that now and then ruffled her hair, making it seem alive. For a few moments I wasn't there. Afterward I heard Capasso again, the third not yet, he said. And my father: "Get away from here."

"Yes, there are too many people, go on," the marshal ordered. Then to him: "What were you thinking, bringing your daughter."

He looked at the prints in an area where the earth was soft: the horseshoes again, and the cleated sole of a large shoe.

So I found myself with Dario, a few meters farther on. We sat on the ground. He took off the headlamp and put it between us.

"Where's Tania?" I asked.

"Behind that beech. I had also passed by Virginia, but I didn't see her."

He shook his head above the light. They were blaming the animals and yet.

"Where could Doralice be?"

Nearby no, they had all searched. No one even knew if she had been with them. Or maybe she'd managed to escape.

"But from whom?"

"Someone on a horse, I think."

He offered me a licorice and I took it, but then I couldn't put it in my mouth. We sat there, me with the black lozenge in my hand and between us the little light pointed at the sky. We were young but not invincible. We were fragile. I discovered in an instant that we could fall, get lost, and even die.

That night Dario and I were close for the first time. Occasionally the voices of the men around Virginia reached us, information crackling from the radio. The magistrate was coming up on foot. A few paces from us: stay strong, my father said to Osvaldo, who was leaning on a rock. I had never seen a grown man, his face lined by tears, with that fear in his eyes.

He seemed to yield to his own height, the strong bone structure he was proud of. I never again saw my father console someone the same way.

Every so often I looked at the police, and her in the midst of them, to remind myself that it had really happened. All that evil, come to where Doralice and I had played hide-and-seek as children, our lips stained with strawberries. We'd put them in big, bowl-like leaves. For my father it was the safest place in the world. Safer than the crowded bus that carried me to the sea, or the beach with the near-naked people. For him the dangers were down there. Instead his woods had betrayed him.

He turned, in disbelief. At times my thoughts summoned him. In those hours he had lost all his certainties; he stared at me as if I could explain to him such a death.

"He must have attacked them from the horse, and they couldn't defend themselves," Dario said.

He had found a girl's body, by himself, in the dark. He was stricken, but not as much as me. Sometimes, over the years, I've thought back to his strength that night at Pietra Rotonda.

nother light was moving toward us. Here he is, the marshal said. He wasn't expecting a prosecutor like that: a woman in jeans and hiking boots was walking briskly beside an officer. Capasso greeted her, and she introduced herself: Grimaldi. Before Virginia she stiffened for a moment, then observed her for a long time, from different angles. Now and then Dario and I could hear her voice clearly, in that silence.

"Someone out of control," she said to the marshal.

With her, the scene changed. She had the girls covered, and said they shouldn't be left alone.

"They could be eaten by animals."

The area was marked off, she indicated the perimeter to the officer who was stretching the tape from tree to tree. She questioned Dario, near Tania. She asked if she was still warm when he found her. And earlier, while he was searching, had there been shots in the woods? The magistrate spoke louder, to everyone. "Be careful, he's armed and has nothing to lose. He could be hiding around here."

Capasso had asked for reinforcements, we heard him on the radio: police were arriving from the entire region. They would look for Doralice and a murderer. Agents from Forensics were coming from Rome. That long night was rushing to its end. In me a painful tumult, but I was also excited: the inconceivable was happening.

"I didn't understand anything—he killed them with a gun," Dario said when he stepped over the tape.

My father had understood but had said nothing. A hunter recognizes gunshot wounds. Those bloodstains on their bodies.

We had to get away from there, it was dangerous. I went over to my father, I needed his protection. At times I'd found him ridiculous with the gun over his shoulder, but right then it reassured me; he had carried it to Pietra Rotonda as well. So we set out toward the campground, he and Osvaldo in front, then Dario and I. I left without separating from Virginia's body, so motionless and white. I didn't want to believe that the girls couldn't get up, return to the morning, relive differently the last day of their vacation. A brief delay would have been enough, another half hour of sleep in the safety of the tent, or not taking that path. A small deviation and they would have escaped the encounter. Even today I don't understand how they could have been at that exact point, in the vastness of the mountain. They had an appointment set by chance.

A reporter who'd reached the place trailed behind us, complaining about Grimaldi, who had expelled him at the first camera flash. He, too, was working. Then he started with questions: What were we doing there, were we relatives of the victims? Had another girl really disappeared? We tried to keep him away from Osvaldo, who lengthened his stride in order not to hear him.

In *Quotidiano Adriatico* the next day he inserted doubts about Grimaldi: a woman with not many years of experience in the judiciary, assigned to follow such a brutal crime. Print and television, regional and not, were constantly criticizing her, even after the trial.

We didn't let the reporter get near the Sheriff. He stuck around, wandering here and there, snapping some photos. He wanted to know who the campground belonged to, but we didn't tell him.

That same morning Grimaldi returned to the prosecutor's office and opened a case against unknown persons, charging multiple homicide and sexual assault. She entered the injured parties.

She later inserted in the file the police log, in which it was reported that: Osvaldo Damiani had appeared before them at 11:45 P.M. on August 28 1992 along with a friend of his daughter Doralice, to report the disappearance of the same. She hadn't returned at the usual time to the family campground, in the locality of Dente del Lupo. The last time she was seen she was wearing black pants and a short-sleeved yellow shirt. A squad was led to the place, where the undersigned marshal Andrea Capasso received news of the body of a girl found in the locality of Pietra Rotonda. Arriving there, he reported the presence of the dead body on the ground, in a supine position, with a bloodstain on the chest. She was immediately identified as Tania Vignati, by means of the ID card acquired at the campground where she was staying. Around thirty meters away a second dead body was found, half naked, hit by several gunshots to the chest and abdomen. Presumably it was the sister, Virginia, also from Bomporto (MO). No trace of Doralice Damiani in the same place.

8.

Did anyone know where the Trignani farm was? The call came from there. The sergeant was asking the volunteers and the curious who had stationed themselves between the *casotto* and the campground. The sky above Dente del Lupo was beginning to lighten when he got the call. The hamlet of Colledoro, he specified, but no one knew that farm. It was in another locality, in the direction of Teramo, it must be eight kilometers if not ten, they answered. I more or less know the road, Osvaldo said, then we'll ask which house. He was ready to leave.

He drank a coffee in one gulp, the Sheriff had made it when we came down from Pietra Rotonda. At first she wept for Virginia and Tania, for their parents, who might already be on their way. Then she recovered herself: her daughter hadn't been found. She might be alive. She went over to the Madonna of the Seven Swords.

"You can understand me," she prayed, staring at the painted figure. "She's all I have, save her."

She stayed there for a while, hands entwined. Every so often she shook them, asking without voice: What are you doing? Give her back to me. Then she started moving again, mechanically. She brought the grandfather bread and orzo, insulted the reporter, who was annoying her.

Ciarango also drank the Sheriff's coffee, *corretto,* with sambuca. He hadn't been up at Pietra Rotonda much. To the marshal he had said that his was only a work horse, it transported the milk cans. He'd kept him quiet since he'd gone lame. And then he wasn't the only horse in the area, other shepherds had horses, too.

At the last minute Ciarango went over to the Alfetta that was leaving for Colledoro. He knew where the Trignanis were, he had sold them a lamb at Easter. He explained to the sergeant where to get off the highway, how to recognize the farm. It wasn't so easy. There was a small white church before you got to it.

"Come with us," my father said.

Osvaldo got in the Ritmo, leaving him the front seat. Ciarango shook his head a little and got in.

For several days my father kept to himself what happened between them on the way to the Trignani farm. Then one night after dinner he told my mother everything. He spoke in a low voice, with a kind of embarrassment, but I heard him.

"You can fool the police, not people who've known you a lifetime."

It was Osvaldo who started off.

What do you mean, the other asked him.

"No one here has a horse, only you. I saw the fresh hoof-prints with my own eyes."

He was certainly ungrateful, Ciarango responded. A person loses sleep to help him find his daughter and here's the thanks. Did he want to fight?

"Stop it," my father said, but they didn't even hear him.

"Some help you are. You're not saying what you know."

That's enough, my father repeated, while he tried to stay be-hind the police. Neither one would give up the last word.

"It's my business where the horse is. I don't have to account to someone who's ordered around by his wife."

At that point Osvaldo jumped up from the seat, grabbed him by the neck, and squeezed. It was you, it was you, he shouted in his ear. Whether it was a question or a certainty wasn't clear.

Ciarango, taken by surprise, tried to free himself, struck blindly. Insults and curses were strangled in his throat. His beard protected him in part, in part a sudden braking. My father pushed Osvaldo back: you're crazy, he said. They calmed down, breathing hard. When they started off again, they could no longer see the Alfetta. Around a few more bends and there it was, waiting for them. They passed it before the turn for Colledoro.

"Tomorrow I'm going to report you," Ciarango said to Osvaldo.

Then he went on talking to my father, as if the other weren't there. Every so often he massaged his neck, digging for it under the beard.

"I gave the horse to Vasile, to go up to the high pastures."

The two cars came out of the woods and it was morning. At the crossroads Ciarango guided them by gestures, along roads between steep fields. They passed the church, and right afterward he pointed to the farm. Doralice had made it there, wounded but alive.

DENTE DEL LUPO

1.

The woman with the frozen shoulder should be in the waiting room, but she's late today, too. Then she complains about the pain: and will it take much longer to release? It's my father who rang, I find him sitting beside the window. When he appears in the office without warning I'm on the alert.

"There's no one here today—you don't have much work?" he starts off.

It's only a patient who's late, I reassure him. He's wearing a shirt I've never seen, white with a blue legend: NAVIGARE. It makes me smile, to think of ships on the chest of someone who has seen them only on TV. What's he doing here, I ask.

"You haven't come lately, I came."

I remind him that we had lunch on Thursday, just four days ago. Oh yes, he says, it seemed to him longer. If it was up to him I'd be there all the time, cleaning the house and helping him in the garden. Or it's only a little company he's looking for. Someone to exchange a few words with: a neighbor, a relative, his daughter.

He came by to say hello, he explains, since he had to go to the pharmacy at the corner. And he brought me some new potatoes, he points to an old shopping bag.

"This year I planted the ones Osvaldo gave me, they have more flavor."

I believe it, I respond with a nod.

"By any chance have you two met?" he resumes, cautiously.

I haven't seen Osvaldo. But he may have to talk to you, says my father. Someone is interested in Dente del Lupo.

"You're always thinking about the campground. Is that why you're here?"

No, he came to bring me the potatoes, he insists. Amanda helped him dig them yesterday. She came by to visit and he put her to work with hoe and wheelbarrow. She had been at the mountain, he thought I knew. My daughter doesn't tell me where she's going?

She doesn't tell me, for the little she goes out. And then I left early yesterday, we went to sing in the Marche. It seems to him too far. What's the point of the chorus? It doesn't even pay. I could rest on Sunday.

"That's how I rest. And they even gave us a prize, after the concert."

He's never liked music, he looks at me skeptically, as if he'd seen the silver plaque we got. I look at him, too, in the boy's T-shirt that Rubina, seeing it on him, would find "cool." He must have bought it at the store that sells the cargo pants. But that word is stirring some anger in me. He never wanted to hear about the sea, and when the doctor recommended it to my mother for her bones, he made no effort to take her. Let's try it, she begged him, it's not as if we have to be undressed. The sun you get in the country is enough, he said. Then, with her brittle bones, she fractured a vertebra. My father has never plowed anything but his land.

The patient arrived breathless, muttering excuses, a tractor wouldn't let her pass. She and my father greet each other, they meet sometimes at the greenhouse. She buys flowers, he tomatoes. I'm an old man, he says to her, to hear her respond no, you're so youthful. He gets up, stops a moment in the doorway: "Listen to what Osvaldo wants, then."

If Osvaldo has to talk to me he knows where to find me, and I turn my back. The woman lies down on the table and I start palpating the muscles. She has stiffened around her pain; first I treat the scapula. My father's words return: Osvaldo, Amanda digging potatoes, Dente del Lupo.

It seems to me unlikely that anyone could be interested in the campground today. Maybe it's people from outside, who don't know the story. They don't know that the spirits of the two girls still roam the woods. Sometimes I imagine them wandering at night, without respite, all the way to Pietra Rotonda. For months those voices carried by the wind robbed the people in the valley of their sleep. The misfortunes of the place began with them, that wound couldn't heal. For a long time the road was cut off by a landslide, Dente del Lupo has disappeared from the tourist guides, and no one goes to walk its paths. I have no idea why Amanda went back up there.

"More gently, please," says the patient.

2

The boy sitting opposite me is writing numbers and symbols on a graph-paper pad. I recognize that sort of long S of the integrals, it's a not exactly pleasant memory of my fifth year in high school. He bumps me with his foot and apologizes, I ask if he's studying mathematics. It hurts me to see him so absorbed by his formulas, it hurts me for Amanda. In the afternoon she'd solve the problems assigned by Professor Ferri with the same absorption, bent over her notebook in a past that seems so distant.

The train isn't the same as it was the other time; my mood is different. Then I was taking her to seize hold of her adult life. I would miss her, but hope for her future was stronger than the longing I felt for her. Today I'm going to get the remains of her life in Milan. Dario and I talked on the phone, it seemed pointless to continue paying the rent. She removed herself: I'm not going back there even for a moment, she said. You go and get the few things left, if you really want to. Summer has burned the plain that seen through the window two years ago was green.

The agency is in a hurry to get the keys, have the room available. Let the next one come on, four hundred euros a month for the single room; Amanda was only an extra.

I would have liked to study medicine, but the course was too long and expensive for my parents. I didn't ask myself too many questions. I was satisfied with three years of physiotherapy and I've loved my work. I leased a studio and escaped from the countryside, from my father: I didn't end up packing chicken breasts at the poultry plant. Now I treat some of the workers, their hands ruined by the damp cold of the refrigerated rooms. What will Amanda do?

The boy lowers his mask and eats a sandwich, with his hand sweeps up the crumbs that fall on the integrals.

I find the apartment silent, no one's there in this period. The room is dark because of the lowered blinds, I open the window and rather than light an opaque air enters. I expected disorder, the bed unmade; Amanda left in a hurry before the city closed down. A confusion of shoes and, far apart, the boiled-wool slippers I gave her. But the books are in place, lined up on the shelf. There's not one on the table; I doubt whether my daughter studied in here. Instead there are pizza boxes containing dried crusts, pieces of bread crumbled in her way, empty cans. In the closet there's not much to take away. Empty and clean, the woman at the agency said on the phone. I look for what I need in the broom closet and begin.

"Are you Amanda's mother?"

The voice makes me jump, the rustling of the garbage bag covered the footsteps. I nod and shake a can before throwing it in. She's not the same girl I saw the other time, this one has glasses and long hair. She's sorry Amanda didn't come back, but quite a few of them are continuing to study from home. I don't know how to answer her, I nod again, weakly. And anyway she understands if Amanda wants to move. I put a crust in the bag, here we separate the garbage, she observes. Of course, also where I am—I was distracted for a moment. I go back to the cans.

"I was there that night," she says, and I ask: what night?

"When she was attacked."

The girl comes a little closer, a white-gold V shines in the décolleté of her shirt. She'd been studying with earplugs, because of the noise from the floor above. She didn't hear the bell ringing and ringing. Amanda tried the other bells, too, but no one opened the door. Maybe they weren't home, or didn't want to open. And then it was late, Amanda was coming back from a concert. She remained outside alone, in the cold, wounded.

"Maybe an hour, or more. Every so often she tried again, but I didn't hear her until I took out the earplugs."

She was shocked when she saw the blood, but didn't say anything, so as not to frighten her even more. She lent her the phone and went back to studying, it was only a few hours until her exam.

"But Amanda kept saying she was fine."

Anyway she was lucky, she adds. In what sense, I ask. In the sense that it was only a robbery, they didn't do anything else to her. What do you mean, I'd like to say, and yet I'm silent. She's right, they could have done worse to my daughter.

Her gaze falls on the cups, the box of plum cake open on the nightstand.

"After that she changed," she says. "She stopped eating with me and the others."

She went out for classes and that's all, then not even for those. Certainly at home she'll feel better. I don't answer, so that I'm not always lying.

I still have to understand my daughter's trouble, it doesn't come from just one place. It began here, maybe the city was too harsh for her. For a moment I'm tempted to confide in this girl, tell her about Amanda, how she is now. But what's the point, I don't even know her name, if the V of the charm is for Valeria, Valentina, or Veronica. She didn't introduce herself, and if Amanda told me I've forgotten. I look at her, she can't do anything for us.

"If you need something I'm here. My name is Viola."

3.

Amanda could have taken refuge here that night. She had only to turn right at the end of the street, then it's a hundred meters. She must have known the café, she passed it to get the metro at the Lodi TIBB station. They would have welcomed her, helped her, the Chinese owner is nice. What time do you close, I ask the waiter who serves me breakfast. At ten, signora. Too early.

Lazily I taste the foam of the cappuccino. Why didn't I understand right away what she suffered? Where was I while she was cold and fearful at the building's entrance? It's the fate of mothers: a time comes when they are no longer able to protect their children.

The ringing woke me with a start, the remote fell out of my hands. I was lying on the couch, the TV still on. I made light of what had happened, I wanted to reassure her. I didn't go to her the next morning.

"You didn't sleep," Dario says, sitting down.

He found me right away, I sent him the address of the café. From a distance a nod of greeting: he always walks like a person in the mountains.

I couldn't sleep last night, in the bed that for a short time was Amanda's. Her unquiet breath was between the sheets, her pacing back and forth in an alien room. Cleaning it, I got the impression that she never liked it. Her insomnia that night and perhaps countless others infected me. I swallowed the melatonin I found on the nightstand without looking at the expiration date, and still couldn't sleep.

"You can tell? And yet I did put on makeup," and I touch with my fingers the masked circles under my eyes.

The last time I saw him at home, he brought a birthday present for our daughter. She appeared a little sullen and didn't open the package, which held a new tablet; she put it on a chair. But she gave him a kiss when he left.

Dario orders a coffee, at nine in the morning it's already his second, he reproaches himself. He had one on the highway. It's warmer here, he observes. He looks a little speeded up to me, sitting in the chair but as if he were about to jump to his feet. I ask him about work. He's just been made manager of an important branch, he answers, with a touch of satisfaction.

"Then it was worth the trouble," I say.

"What?"

"To move to Turin."

The other question I had for him no longer makes sense. If there was the possibility of being closer. Geographically, I meant. And maybe also to me. I swallow it.

How was our daughter's room, he wants to know. Rather topsy-turvy. And there's only one girl there.

"Did she tell you anything about Amanda?"

That she wasn't happy in Milan. Maybe she didn't even like what she was studying.

"And you didn't notice anything?"

"Why, did you notice something?"

It was to me that Amanda returned for vacations.

"I wasn't there," he defends himself.

Precisely, he wasn't there and I had to understand everything from the silences? A pause and then Dario asks me.

"Is it my fault?"

I shrug. Impossible to answer him with a yes or no. I don't know how to divide the blame. And I don't know if Amanda's choices still depend on us. At a certain point we lose our grip on our children's lives. They go off on their own and look at us without pity.

When her father left for Turin, she told me we were separating. He left you and you didn't even notice, so she said. She wasn't wrong. On the weekend I talked to him at a distance, sometimes lighthearted, laughing on the phone at imitations of his colleagues. He didn't make video calls; I never saw the apartment around his voice. He was distant, but he was always part of me. I suffered his absence in silence. And he came home again, those few times.

In her first months in Milan she went to see him on the train, but she told me nothing about her father, about his life in the city. She spoke to me only about the restaurants in which they ate agnolotti and *vitel tonné*. Then they stopped meeting.

Last night, like her, I ordered pizza, to be delivered, and ate it on the table in the room. It was already cut in slices, I took them out of the box and chewed slowly.

I'm not angry with Amanda, I'm worried about her. Dario is, too, it's clear. He sighs and drinks his coffee, pays for my breakfast, too. We set out toward the building, he left the car in front. Going up to the fourth floor we exchange only glances that immediately turn away. I've gotten everything ready that we have to take away. Those I threw out: the condoms I found in the back of the drawer in the nightstand. I opened the box of eighteen, five were missing. Someone spent time with her, they had sex in the single bed. The secret life of children. We know it exists but we're never ready to touch it. In the closed space of our heads they remain sexless angels forever. Undifferentiated, never completely born.

Last night Viola gave me a box to put the books in. Dario takes one out, turns it over in his hands, looks at the shiny cover.

"They're new. Amanda must have done some exams?"

I think so, at first. She talked to me about them. But you

checked, he insists. There's no way of checking, she's an adult. And then what's the use, now she's decided to drop out.

"That's not definite. We can find a place in a safer neighborhood."

I recognize his stubbornness, it will have no effect on Amanda. It's important to him for his daughter to get a degree, he won't give in. He doesn't know how resistant she's become.

We're squeezed into the elevator with the bags, the box of books. A sadness without hope grips us both. Third floor, second, first, and ground. Dario fiddles in the trunk, we won't hear anything shift during the trip. We go back up to the room, to see if we've forgotten anything. It's empty, no trace of Amanda's passage. The woman from the agency finds the keys on the table, looks around, the room is clean, all right. She checks only the closet doors, to make sure that they're not broken, and that the blind goes up and down without getting stuck. We stay a few more minutes, I knock on Viola's door. Say hi to Amanda, she says. "I've written to her a few times, but she doesn't respond to messages."

I wish her good luck and she thanks me with fingers crossed. She expects to graduate in October. The world has never been so full of people studying.

We leave, and once we're on the highway Dario finds his voice again.

"One of these Saturdays I'll come and get my last things. I'll free up the closet."

"So it's final?"

He shrugs. It's already happened, there's nothing new, he says. It's true, but while we give a name to what has already happened I feel faint.

"Your sweaters don't bother me."

He knows it, but in Turin they'll be more useful. I can't find an intelligent remark to stop him before the final rupture. Now it's late, he reproaches me. It's not even a reproach, there's too much indifference.

"You haven't come even once to see where I am."

"I have a job," I remind him.

"But you work for yourself," he points out. "If you want to extend the weekend by a day you can afford it. You promised you'd come. You didn't even make the effort."

At first he expected me, he says, from week to week. I'd like the city, maybe I'd be persuaded to join him with Amanda. Slowly he got used to it. He doesn't miss me anymore. I look at him, desolate, without defending myself.

"You've stayed more closely tied to your father than to me. You can't get away from there."

I'm the only child, I remind him, my father is old and ill. I have a moral obligation to help him.

"Exactly, you made your choice."

"You also made your choice: your career."

He should have done it long ago, he says. He stayed all those years to be with us. Amanda and me.

Our eyes meet in the empty space between the seats, while the tires beat against the joints of a viaduct. *Ta-tan, ta-tan.* I lack the will to respond, he's not wrong, not completely. We're losing each other like this, without passion and without blood.

I don't know for how many kilometers we're silent. Then the tone is different, hard but also light.

"By the way, could you ask your father if he'll come get you at the Ancona exit?"

"He doesn't want to drive on the highway anymore. You could have said it before and I would have taken the train."

"And all that stuff in the back?"

"You could take it to Turin. Amanda doesn't want any of it."

4.

Amanda and I ran into them in front of the entrance, just today when I had persuaded her to come to the supermarket with me. You can help me with the heavier things, I said, and she: what things, it's only you and me. I don't know how many days since she'd been out, I don't even count them anymore. The sunlight wounded her, she protected her eyes with her arm. And in the sun were these two, they were looking for me. Osvaldo introduced us to the man, who had a vigorous handshake: a pleasure, Gerí.

Now they're sitting on my couch. They were on the mountain this morning, such peace up there, says Gerí, such beauty. As a young man he used to come from Pescara for the Sheriff's *arrosticini*, what a woman. They've been friends since, he and Osvaldo. Friends who are different, it seems to me: at least ten years separates them and the watch I see on Gerí's wrist is worth at least twice as much as the Ape. He also spent a few nights at the campground once, he recalls. A pity how run-down it is now.

"Your father and I talked, did he tell you that Gerí's interested in the land?" Osvaldo interrupts.

"Not really, no," I say. "He only mentioned something, without naming anyone."

My father—that's what he was alluding to the other day in the office.

"But I knew you'd stop by."

He'd wanted to come, but he took the opportunity of this

walk up to Dente del Lupo and brought Gerí in person. And my property interests this man with the expensive watch.

"At the moment my company is looking for a place like that."

But to do what, I ask, bewildered. They still don't know precisely, maybe a resort, maybe enlarge the campground, adding structures, tent platforms, enhancing it to fit the requirements of today's clientele. As he talks his hands lay out in the air the new structures and platforms. And that pool, so small—his fingers enlarge it in an instant.

"You can't build there."

I nearly jump at the sound of Amanda's harsh voice behind me. We all three turn toward her.

"Maybe you don't know the land is protected," she says. And to Osvaldo: "You abandoned the campground for all these years and now you're thinking of fixing it by pouring concrete?"

I had lost sight of her, I thought she'd gone to her room. She's leaning against the wall, apart, but her voice cuts the space. "People like you two are always trying."

They ignore her, waiting for her to finish. But Osvaldo is uneasy, he's studying his shoes.

"Grandfather gave that place to you, Mamma. It's up to you to protect it."

Reaching me now the sound is warm: the last time she called me mamma is so long ago.

The echo of her words hovers in the air, comes to rest on the floor, the carpet, the shoulders of us adults. It leaves us in silence.

"The permits exist. But the deadline is coming up," Osvaldo says then.

I'm still silent, although those two are expecting a response, at least a signal of willingness or the opposite. Gerí's idea seems unrealizable to me, and I don't understand Osvaldo, so taken with his role as middleman. But now I understand my father's rush to leave me the land: he didn't want to get mixed up in this business, as they say. He'd known from the start, certainly. He mixed me up in it instead.

"You saw that the place isn't in the tourist guides anymore?"

Gerí is unperturbed, on the contrary. People now are looking for just that, isolated places, far from the crowd. An experiential tourism. He stumbles for a moment on the word. I also stumble, asking Osvaldo if he and my father talked about experiential tourism at Dente del Lupo. He stares at me expressionless, it's not worth the effort, what we're saying is incomprehensible and doesn't concern him.

"Think about it, you don't have to answer now. You'll be getting an offer from me soon."

I turn in search of Amanda, she's no longer there. She moves in the house without a sound.

Gerí gets up, thanks me for my time. I wait at the window to see them in the street, they're heading toward a black BMW. They gesticulate, talking about Amanda and me, I imagine. Next to that car is another one that doesn't belong to anyone here. I would recognize it among a thousand similar cars: the treble clef stamped on the back makes it unique. Is it the first time the maestro has been to see Rubina or did I not notice before? She's always telling me, about what happens in the town: you're the only one who doesn't know. They're together two floors below, maybe they're having a coffee and that's all, or talking about the next concerts. I find it unlikely. It's as if I were jealous, but for no reason. After all for me Milo is only the director of the chorus. Maybe I envy Rubina, who at sixty still seizes hold of life.

I call Amanda through the door of her room. It's late now, she says, she won't come to the supermarket. The intention has expired, by paying attention to those two men I lost the moment I'd caught. She's so changeable, my daughter, her awakenings are brief.

I have no desire to go out, either. My father, on the phone, isn't surprised that Osvaldo came over with that Gerí. You didn't by chance know about it, I ask. He never knew anything. And then what's the harm, he didn't eat me, he only wanted to meet. In fact tomorrow he'll send me an email with an offer for the land. My father's amazed: for thirty years no one wanted it, and in a day an offer arrives.

But he didn't know about it, I insist, he didn't talk to Gerí. I hear him rummaging with his free hand in something or other, he goes away for a moment and returns. He's a big shot, he says, he owns the two biggest hotels on the coast. He can't pronounce the foreign names, but I must have seen them passing by.

"You would sell him Dente del Lupo?" I ask.

He would never sell land, and never that, which belonged to his grandfather. Just thinking of it would break his heart. He's never found a place like that anywhere, he says, as if he'd traveled the world. Besides the campground there's the woods and then the gently sloping field, with the age-old beech in the middle. It refreshes you just to look at it. I didn't think my father had a sense of beauty different from the useful.

"But Osvaldo is always desperate, with Gerí's money he'd get back on his feet."

What does Osvaldo gain, he's not the owner, I remind him. He gains, he gains. Then I hear him shifting something, hammering. He holds the phone between shoulder and ear, he can't stand still. You have to decide, *bang*. That's why I left you Dente del Lupo, *bang bang*. He stops, silence for a moment.

"I don't want to get old, but it's happening."

Another pause and then: "I can't do anything for Osvaldo. You help him, if you feel like it."

He's banging on thin metal, *ting ting*.

5

S ometimes I wish I played an instrument less human than
my voice. A violin, say, which would always be the same,
at every rehearsal, every concert, except for the vagaries
due to temperature and humidity. I'd be able to tune it better
than I can tune myself. But I didn't study music, and now it's
too late. I have this voice that changes with mood. The other
night we rehearsed in the cathedral: in the high empty nave
the singing was lost. It seemed to me that I got there only with
an effort. And the director was too harsh, reprimanding me
in front of everyone. Usually he goes up to each person and
whispers corrections. He was impatient the other night, and I
wasn't focused enough in the Kyrie. At one point he snapped at
all of us: even if you're an amateur chorus you can't allow this
sloppiness, he said. Some moments of silence, then from the beginning, with more conviction. Finally in the last minutes I loos-
ened up. Milo approved with a nod. At home later my throat
felt scratchy. Rubina came up with her vial and counted out for
me all those drops of hedge mustard in half a glass of water.

Today we're singing at the eleven o'clock Mass in the basilica of Collemaggio. Some of us hadn't been to L'Aquila since
the earthquake. Samira not before, either, and she's almost
ashamed. She sat next to me on the bus, she took a day off, so
as not to miss it. I ask her about the hotel where she works, is it
by any chance one of the two owned by Gerí?

"Spezzaferro, you mean?"

I thought Gerí was his last name, but it turns out to be his first name. When she hears it, Samira's face darkens. No, she works at the reception desk of a smaller hotel, not far away. She had tried at the Long Beach when she was in school, supporting herself on seasonal jobs. Once, at the start of the summer, she went for a job interview. A blonde was in charge of personnel, but he was also in the office, on the phone. The woman showed him the form with Samira's information, he looked at it distractedly, still talking on the phone. The woman stood there, waiting. Finally he pointed to something on the form, they exchanged a glance. I'm sorry, we don't need anyone, the woman had said to Samira, giving her back the form. But there was the sign outside: CHAMBERMAIDS WANTED. Oh yes, she had forgotten to take it down.

"They saw my name and wouldn't hire me," Samira says.

She smiles sardonically at my disbelief. It wasn't the first time. For people in Pescara you have only to be a Spinelli or a Di Rocco and you're a thief. They're Gypsy surnames.

She asks if I know Spezzaferro.

"He wants to buy some land we have in the mountains."

"Be careful," she warns me. "He's not very well regarded, the other hotel owners complain that he competes unfairly."

At Dente del Lupo he certainly wouldn't find any competitors. Over the years even most of the shepherds have left. Ciarango's pen no longer exists. The opening of the campground annoyed him, all those tourists going around trampling the fields. He of all people called them dirty pigs. He was enraged by the tinfoil from a sandwich thrown on the grass. Sometimes he got angry at my father, who had rented the land to Osvaldo.

"Don't worry," I say to Samira. "I'm not sure we're selling it."

We left an hour early so we'd have time to visit the basilica. The others linger before the façade, I go in. The stripped-down beauty of the restoration surprises me. I sit in a pew and feel welcomed, in my distance from God. The silence calms me, the few visitors are respectful. If I had faith I would now pray to Santa Maria in Collemaggio to help my daughter, to repair her. A Madonna would be able to illuminate that crack in her that I still can't find. She might fill the empty space with meaning.

In one of the frescoes there's a horizontal cavity right at the feet of Christ on the cross, but it's been filled in with plaster. The difference in color is clear, and yet it's not troubling. It means there was a wound, and it healed. I startle at the touch of a hand on my hair. Rubina sits down near me. She's my friend, she's here, her scent envelops me.

After the Mass, the priest compliments our singing. If we'd like, he'll invite us for the Christmas Mass. We'd be happy to come back, the maestro assures him. In this late-summer heat the holidays seem so far away. I wonder if anything in my life will have changed, if Amanda will change at all. Maybe it will be easier to get her out of her room, so that we can sit at the table together on Christmas Eve.

We go out onto the square. The midday light is blinding, highlights the red and white of the façade. Milo comes over, he says that today he liked my singing, truly.

"You seemed inspired, as if you were praying."

On the bus I turn the phone back on. The message from a patient who postpones tomorrow's appointment irritates me, he's constantly doing that. I'm not going to call him to make a new one. I also open my email, one has arrived. Punctually, even though it's Sunday, the Spezzaferro group has written to me. Here he is, Gerí. In the subject line his best offer for purchase of the land called Dente del Lupo. He knows it better than I do, not even the notary's documents reported all these details: area in hectares, parcels, names and surnames of the adjacent owners. Even the distance from the state road is there: two hundred meters. Gerí has made a thorough study of what he wants to get.

6

He asked me to help Osvaldo and then added: if you feel like it. If you love him is what my father means. He doesn't know the words of affection, his vocabulary doesn't include them. Occasionally I think of him as a young man, who didn't know how to talk about love to a girl having her first and only experience. Maybe she expected a partial declaration in dialect. They conceived me mutely, he out of ignorance, she out of modesty.

Between men there was no need for talk, he and Osvaldo were friends in hunting, in haying, in certain reckless drunken episodes that they still describe to one another. They helped each other without caring who gave or took more. One held the head of the lamb, the other cut its throat with a sharp stroke. They both ate it, no longer remembering whose lamb it had been alive.

I don't know precisely how Osvaldo got into debt, or how the debts grew over time. My father always blamed the swimming pool, which alone cost more than the whole campground. The small excavator that could get up there was rented by the day, and at a high price. Then he had to pay the worker who operated it and someone else to truck the earth and rocks off the mountain. A second excavation was needed to bring up the water pipes. It seemed they would never finish.

At home my father said that Osvaldo was taking a risky step, but it was too late to stop now. Now he's there. We really couldn't do without a hole in the field, the shepherds said behind his back. Leave it be, after a season the animals will be drinking from it. For a long time they watched the bucket as it bit the earth.

It must have been then that Osvaldo started asking for loans from this one and that, a million lire from an uncle, two from a friend. From my father five, I think, they were closer. My mother muttered her disagreement, but she wasn't the one to decide. She never went to see the excavation, and maybe not even the finished job.

In good times there weren't enough campsites, the tents were practically piled on top of one another, and the Sheriff's incomparable *arrosticini* summoned people to the *casotto* across the way. The pool, so high up, also attracted people, including me. It was fun to mix in with the tourists. I swam with them and sometimes passed for one. From the edge Doralice searched among the wet heads for mine. I can see her blinking, dazzled by the reflections of the sun on the water. Osvaldo was satisfied, a crazy idea of his wife's had become reality and prospered. Small debts accumulated, but he felt he had the energy to honor them to the last. The pool functioned for only two summers. It was still new in that August that overturned the future.

The campground reopened the next year, but the weather was immediately against it. June was rainy: in the mountains it seemed like November but green. In July an unprecedented wind swept away the two solitary pup tents pitched at Dente del Lupo. My father chased after them, while they flew off to get stuck on the angry foliage of the beeches. He gave Osvaldo a hand when he could. Those four campers were so frightened that they left at sunset, recovering a small part of what the gusts had carried off. Without the Sheriff the place wasn't the same, but she was adamant, she wouldn't go back. Osvaldo tried to reopen the *casotto*, by himself, along with a kid who waited on the tables. His *arrosticini* were raw one moment and burned the next, his wife's perfect cooking forever eluded him. People would go there to eat one night, and weren't seen again.

Some years ago I met them, my father and Osvaldo, in the bank. Not met, exactly. Your father's in there, a cashier said to me, not very attentive to privacy. She indicated a door, I knew it was the loan office. And what's he doing there, I asked. My father had no need of a loan. She shrugged: he's with a man, they're signing. Osvaldo must have exhausted the circle of acquaintances he could approach.

I waited in the square for them to come out. They didn't see me, they went away together, talking. I was immediately sure: my father was guaranteeing the loan with the house and land, what he loved most in the world. He was capable of that, for his friend. Every so often he also gave him money to pay the bills, my mother told me, shaking her head, when she was still able to understand. As if we had extra, she said. But the two of them also managed to put aside some of their pension: they spent little thanks to the garden, the chickens, and the rabbits. Osvaldo's debts, instead, have multiplied over the years, and maybe the Sheriff doesn't know all of them. Creditors harbor weak, persistent grudges. They talk to one another, how much does he owe you, and on those lips Osvaldo is no longer the tall straight man he once was.

My father is asking me to help him. He feels for him, he's sorry for him. I'm sure that Doralice doesn't suspect any of her parents' difficulties, it's important to them that she find everything in order when she returns. Her father doesn't ask her, it would be too humiliating.

I open the email again, I skim the text quickly, down to the figure. I reread it several times, I count the zeroes. I don't believe in the sixty thousand euros that Gerí Spezzaferro is offering. It's more than twice what I expected for land full of rubble, as my father calls it. He, especially, won't believe it. You read it wrong, he'll say. No one gives you anything.

7

I couldn't send him away. He came without an appointment, X-rays and reports in one hand, the other on a wooden cane. In his right hip a pain he could no longer endure. He limped as he crossed the short distance of the waiting room to come and talk to me.

"You're Rocco's daughter, your father's a friend of mine. I'll wait, you have to do something for me."

I hadn't seen him in years, but I recognized him. He's the oldest of the shepherds, my father respects him.

"OK, later this morning, after the patients with appointments."

He preferred to sit rather than wander around in this condition. I went back to the woman lying on the table, trying to think if I could put someone off so as not to keep him there too long. The boy at noon took care of it by cancelling his session.

So Achille is lying on my table, at noon. I read his diagnosis, femoral-head necrosis, articular effusion. The orthopedist prescribes magnetotherapy and ultrasound, for now.

"It had to happen to me, I'm always walking with the sheep."

How many does he still have, I ask, positioning the solenoid on the hip. Fifty, now. He never left them, it's always been his job.

"Your father's a good friend to me, he lets me graze his land and never takes money. I try to pay him back in cheese."

It's the best I've eaten, I tell him. I set the timer and listen to him. Now we have to fight, and he has to get back on his feet right away. These devices don't work miracles, I warn him.

"Fight for what?" I ask.

They're planning a protest. By themselves the shepherds aren't enough, they've called on the Greens to organize it. A protest, but where and why? At Dente del Lupo—Achille is surprised I don't know about it. And yet my father was warned. For some time strange people have been going around up there. Some must be surveyors, they're placing their instruments on tripods, taking measurements. Lately they've even fenced some pieces of land. Achille hisses a name between his teeth: it's Gerí, who wants to get the mountain.

The timer sounds the final beep and the solenoid trembles in my hands. Now we go on to the ultrasound, he has to uncover himself a little. How long this time, he asks. Pain or not, he's in a hurry to get back and see what's happening, see if there's any action.

"Your father and Osvaldo never understood anything."

I roll the probe over the skin bathed in conductive gel; the elements of this match begun in spite of me are getting mixed up. The signatures at the notary's, the email from the Spezzaferro group.

"Locked enclosures have never been seen in our area. Now you can't graze there, you can't pick mushrooms."

There's no air, I get up to open the window wider. I have to decide to talk to my father about it. I resume rolling the probe over Achille's sore hip, until he feels some warmth.

"I'm going to go and see," I say.

I've finished the ultrasound, I turn off the device. I look at the schedule, the first patient of the afternoon is someone who gets nervous if there's just a few minutes' wait, but I have to go. I cancel the appointment with a message. Then find me an opening tonight, she answers right away, I can't stand this stiff neck. I write to Amanda to cook and I hurry to Dente del Lupo as if I were losing it. On the way I look in the glove compartment for a candy to trick my empty stomach. Who knows what

Achille meant about Osvaldo. Maybe Gerí has already bought our neighbors' land. But they would have said so when they came to see me. I suck on the Ricola, I drive in doubt.

A line of parked cars extends from the *casotto*, I park at the end and set off toward an excited clamor. On the grass is a flock that has never been so numerous: the shepherds must have brought their sheep together. A banner is attached to the gate of the campground: MOUNTAIN FOR THE SHEPHERDS, SPECULATORS GET OUT. The field is crowded, people are standing there, listening to a man speaking in the tones of a politician about the future of these high terrains. Predatory tourism is not what we need, he says. The passion he puts into it surprises me. A place that was despised, that for thirty years brought bad luck, is suddenly revived and even has a future.

Some people have come from nearby towns as well, a lot of them I don't think I've seen before. I wonder how four old shepherds managed to get all these people together. The aroma of coffee passes by, making me want some. A boy is preparing it in a big pot on a camp stove. Achille gives a statement to local TV.

"For as long as I can remember, the sheep have always grazed where they want."

He's being interviewed by Elsa, a high school classmate of mine. Look down, Achille shouts, and points with his stick to a fenced-off piece of land. A man is there, he waves his hat in response to Achille's nod. He cuts the fence, starts tearing it out. Two shepherds drive the flock in that direction, with whistles, guttural sounds, dogs. Everyone starts down from the field in that direction, Elsa hurries to film the scene. She stumbles on a tuft of grass but doesn't fall, though it's a while since we did gymnastics in the school gym.

Achille is the leader, and every so often he raises his cane, waves it in the air. Has he forgotten his painful hip, or did it not actually hurt so much? I follow at a distance. The opening in the fence widens, the "Private Property" sign falls on the ground. The first sheep to enter trample it, and then, as the crowd applauds, the entire flock streams over the grass. I recognize some people from the town, some from the Alpine Club. Only Osvaldo and my father are missing. I'm afraid of these people, if I sell my part they'll all be against me. A head turns with a flamelike movement. The sun's rays attracted by my daughter's hair. For a moment Amanda smiles—it's a long time since I've seen her teeth so exposed. Those capital A's had something familiar. Maybe she wrote the sign hanging on the campground gate.

8.

After what happened almost everyone except Achille stopped speaking to Ciarango. My father didn't seek him out, but when they met by chance he stopped for a greeting and some remarks on the drought or the low price for the lambs. If Osvaldo was around he confined himself to a nod.

At the trial Ciarango was acquitted of the crime of aiding and abetting, he hadn't hidden the young man. The decision served only to keep him out of jail. He was absolved by the judge in the courtroom, not by those outside.

My father always defended him. It wasn't him, he repeated. Why should he pay for another man's sins?

The summer after the crime the shepherds began to reorganize for the sheep festival at Campo Imperatore. They gathered around the tables at the *casotto*, but no one summoned Ciarango. Achille said it wasn't right to keep him away like that, a man who took first prize every year. At the mere mention of his name, Osvaldo turned red in the face. Doralice then was still spending all her time in her room.

"If he's in I'm out," and Osvaldo got up noisily from his chair.

Next to him was my father, who pulled him down by the arm. He often found himself between the two, sometimes conflicted about whose side to take. In the end Osvaldo always won his heart.

Ciarango seldom came down from the pen now. He ate only cheese and wild fruit, and drank at the springs. His family had given up. His wife would have liked him to come home at least on Saturday, but the clean clothes she left folded on the night-stand remained there for weeks. To anyone who met him in the beechwood, that figure which slowly seemed to be losing human features was frightening.

Another summer came and another, and one morning in June my father went up to the pen. He found him kneeling beside the horse. What have you done, Fulmine, Ciarango mur-mured, running his knotty fingers over the horse's coat. He ca-ressed the old scar, a bear's paw in his face. Fulmine's stomach was swollen and he had a yellowish frothing around his mouth, flies all over him, fierce. He was Ciarango's only companion. When my father leaned over to touch the horse, he was still warm. Together they dug a grave beside that large body, shovel and hoe lost their edge against the rocks. It took hours, in the naked sun of the mountain, sorrow sapped Ciarango's strength. They had to use two wooden stakes as a lever to lower the horse into the ground. Ciarango wept as he covered him.

"He was with you a long time, let him go," my father said.

He wouldn't have believed Ciarango capable of all the tears that bathed his beard.

They didn't see each other in the months after Fulmine's burial. Nor did the other shepherds encounter him in the meadows; he stayed higher up. It was late October when my father went to tell him about someone who was selling a good work horse. Maybe it would interest him. It was very cold in the pen, at the summit a light dusting of snow. Ciarango refused to leave the mountain. He didn't even answer, after Fulmine there was no other for him.

"It's time you came down, you're not a kid anymore."

Those were the last words between them. A few days later, Ciarango's dogs scratched at the door of the house, agitated, whimpering until the sons got moving. Heart attack was the family's version. It seems that they found him hanging by a rope from the beam of the shelter. Nothing definite is known about his end, said my father. I still couldn't believe that the cowboy, as Doralice and I called him, was dead. The spiteful claimed he couldn't have done it by himself. But that was gossip at the bar in the square, fantasies of retired folk who had a lot of time to waste and invented stories between one game of *briscola* and the next.

In the coffin they put his favorite knife, with the horn handle. A well-made suit, beard and hair trimmed.

"Dead he had the face of a Christian again," my father said. "We were all wrong, and he paid for it."

None of the shepherds who are protesting at Dente del Lupo today think about Ciarango anymore or name him. The past twenty years have been hard for them. Many sold their animals, the youngest left to work in the factories. They didn't want to stink of sheep.

The fence is now down on the meadow, the flock grazes free. It fans out, moves toward the campground. I go over to Elsa, who is filming it with her video camera. She stops a moment and looks at me.

"Didn't that campground belong to your father?"

I'm surprised she remembers, she never came to the mountain with us. She doesn't wait for an answer but starts filming, now she's framing Achille, and the crowd, which is moving with him. This place hasn't seen so many people since the night of the crime. After a while those in the valley slept again. They didn't forget; only, they were silent.

One of the shepherds' dogs is getting a little too close. Suddenly I'm tired, with my empty stomach, and the grass around me must be infested with ticks. I'm afraid of the big white dog, of the choice I have to make. I say goodbye to Elsa, who says, Where are you going, wait. I reach the road, and there's my father, he locks the Bravo and puts the key in his pocket.

He heads this way, walking quickly. For a moment rage blurs my vision, he appears out of focus, legs swaying. Calm down, breathe. He looks at the crowd, the sheep, he hasn't seen me.

But, a few meters away, he asks, "What's Achille doing?"

Stay calm, remember he's old. "Achille's protesting," I answer. "He's protesting against Gerí who's buying half the mountain. He'd already put up a fence, see it?"

My tone of voice rises, even though I don't want it to. He observes the torn-up fence, his face expressionless. As usual you didn't know anything, I insist. And then: "You didn't give your word to sell ours, too?"

Now he's close, I can make out the absolute black of his pupils. He stares at me, unruffled. "It's already too much if I keep my word. I'm hardly going to give it for you."

9

Amanda doesn't want to know about the alarm clock. Every night I remind her to set it, she has to have a schedule for getting up, even if it's ten o'clock. Sometimes she listens to me, or pretends to, in order not to hear me. Then in the morning she can ignore it or turn it off, since I'm in my office. At least not on the weekend, she insists, as if for her it weren't always Sunday. We squabble over the alarm clock nearly every night.

"Your bourgeois irritation," she repeats contemptuously. "And yet you're from the countryside."

Precisely. I had to get up early even without a reason. Staying in bed was for spoiled kids, and so get up and breathe the fresh air of dawn.

"You can't make me pay for your childhood," Amanda says.

She gets up only if there's a reason, and she doesn't have one. Hurry up and find one, I reply, and my daughter: fuck off.

Not even instinct helps me with Amanda: rather, it betrays me. I can never relax, I have to push her to stand up, wash, take the garbage down. My push is graceless, sometimes rough. I'm confused myself, I don't know if I'm talking to the child who dawdles or the woman she'll be. But when do children truly begin to be adults? I doubt I'll catch that moment.

Then, unexpectedly, I find her protesting in that field at Dente del Lupo. What's she doing here? Who told her, how did she get here? As usual, I knew nothing about it. She doesn't confide in me.

She's sitting barefoot, legs crossed. She's taking part, but always with that air of a person who's somewhat on her own. The crowd chants in chorus: A-CHIL-LE, A-CHIL-LE. In front of me Elsa is filming them, shepherds and young people. Here's a closeup of Amanda, eyes and hair highlighted. I look at her, too, partly on the screen and partly in reality.

Uh-oh! in my ear makes me jump.

"Isn't that your daughter?"

My father didn't leave, he was wandering around. As if she'd heard him, Amanda turns in this direction, sees us. With her fingertips joined it's she who's asking us: what are you doing here, what do you want. Her grandfather pretends to threaten her, cutting the air with his hand. They're about to carry off Achille in triumph, he says through his teeth. And to me: "What does Amanda have to do with the shepherds?"

He seems more curious than angry with her. Once I asked him why he's so easy on his granddaughter. Because she's not my daughter, he answered. That's me, his daughter. It's been difficult to fight him, and I'm not finished yet. I couldn't always defy him, over time my father has also been right about my life.

Now they're getting up, they head in a group toward the campground, dragging a banner: what in the world have they got in mind. Amanda puts her shoes back on, brushes one of those sticky weeds off her pants. She comes over for a moment, following the flow. What is this nonsense, her grandfather asks, and I, too, with my look.

"Luckily there's Achille, who talks, otherwise I wouldn't have known anything. You didn't tell me everything about this place. You certainly don't have any intention of selling it?"

She's right, neither my father nor I told her about it. We didn't want to think about it anymore. I didn't imagine she'd be interested in what happened then. Maybe I was wrong, Amanda was born here and should know: she should know that piece of our history.

Now, it strikes me, she's teaching us, with her self-important tone, and I like it. She's sending signs of life, a secret life flowing in her. We look at her, moving quickly after the others, then my father and I look at each other.

All these young people at Dente del Lupo, as on summer evenings of talk and beer, when we went up there without a specific date but sure of meeting. We were escaping the suffocating air of the valley: sitting at the Sheriff's tables we let the night go by. Now and then someone pointed to a falling star as it faded out over the peaks.

If Doralice were here I don't think she'd agree with Osvaldo. At some point she must have hated all the shepherds, but so much time has passed. Now maybe she would support Achille. Maybe she no longer feels that tangle of worms swarming underground.

THE FLIGHT

1

There was no one in sight. The farm was still suspended in the morning dampness, a white steam rose from the manure heap. The police checked: the door of the house was closed, the key in the lock and no voices inside. Osvaldo and my father made a circuit of the barn, in search of someone. Ciarango, always behind, stopped to look at a tractor. There, said my father, pointing to where the farmyard ended and became a field, then woods. The woods she'd come from.

They had laid her on a cart, a blanket over her to warm her. The woman cleaned her face and hands with a wet rag. When the rag got red she swished it in a basin of water and wrung it out in her fist. She began to disentangle from her hair a thorny twig that was brushing her forehead. At some point Doralice must have seen the red of her blood, and asked: "Am I going to die?"

She said nothing else, not even to her father, who was leaning over her sobbing.

"No, child, you won't die of this," the woman answered, freeing her from the thorns.

"I'm going out to the road to meet the ambulance, it won't find us here," the husband whispered.

But the police took care of it. They talked to Capasso on the radio. At the Trignani farm, marshal. The wounds don't seem serious but she's in shock. Question her now, no. They have to come from Teramo, we're waiting for them.

Doralice was motionless; at intervals she jerked, and with her the blanket and also the cart, tons of iron.

134 · DONATELLA DI PIETRANTONIO

"Where does it hurt, Dorali'?" Osvaldo asked, squeezing her hand.

No answer, and those eyes staring. Osvaldo moved his index finger in front of her, this side and that, and she didn't follow it. But she took some sips of sugar water that the woman brought to her lips.

My father didn't know how to help his friend in the relief of having found her, in the fear of seeing her like that.

The farm woman didn't forget the girl who arrived in her barnyard at the end of that summer. She had just gotten up and was putting on her socks when she heard the cry: Help, help me.

2

We bought the newspapers for weeks. The van arrived at the newsstand before dawn, unloaded stacks and stacks of papers, tied up with string in a cross. Suddenly the whole town was reading dailies, weeklies, we followed the newscasts on television. Some people saved the pages with the names of our localities. We had never been at the center of any news, least of all crime news. A place like Dente del Lupo became familiar to Italians, the cliff of Pietra Rotonda the set background of reports on the massacre, as they called it. Other reporters preferred to stand in front of the locked gate of the campground, the police seals evident. They pointed inside the enclosure, where Virginia and Tania Vignati had spent their last night in the blue pup tent. But they spoke about the two sisters only briefly, then attention shifted to her, the survivor. In the *Quotidiano Adriatico* she was called "the doe," who had eluded the monster by fleeing through the woods. They sought her out to interview her, both in the hospital and afterward, at home, but the Sheriff wouldn't let them near her daughter. She would have been capable of tearing to pieces anyone who tried it.

Everyone wondered how she had escaped. I also wondered. I was sure that in her place I would be dead. In the darkness I would have surrendered to fear. My mind would have given in to the call of that other mind looking for me.

Some members of the Alpine Club reconstructed Doralice's route through the night: where she had held on to a wall to lower herself, where she had let herself be carried down by the rolling stones of the scree. According to Dario she had passed by the Scaglia, certainly, and, maybe without knowing it, the dens of the wild boars. The moon had faintly illuminated the flight, but also, for the other, the pursuit.

A TV reporter broadcast an exclusive from the Trignani farm. The farmer pointed to the abandoned cart Doralice had leaned against when she let out that cry. Help, and he had turned, had seen her fall to her knees and then to the ground. He imitated the fall in front of the camera. His wife described the wounds, indicating them with her finger on her own arms; she touched her hip where the bullet had gone through Doralice without killing her.

"I thought she might die here, but I gave her courage," she said, pounding with her hand on the iron surface where they'd laid her.

My father had been next to that cart, before the ambulance arrived. He was struck by seeing it again on the screen. He had heard Osvaldo asking his daughter: Who was it? She was silent, eyes staring.

The farm woman said it was by the grace of Santa Colomba that Doralice was alive. As soon as she came out of the woods, the little church had appeared. It was closed, yes, but inside there was that reliquary, and it was powerful. It had protected her from the murderer, had stopped the bleeding. Why the saint hadn't saved the other two girls as well she didn't explain.

In the campground their tent remained up for a couple weeks, by itself. The only family still there the day of the crime had been allowed to leave right after the bodies were found.

My father took care of opening the gate for Tania and Virginia's parents when the seals were removed. It would be better if Osvaldo didn't appear. At the morgue he had tried to approach them. The mother had accepted his condolences, inert, without even understanding who he was. Her husband supported her with one arm.

"You weren't able to protect our daughters," he said to Osvaldo, ignoring the outstretched hand.

With the force of the wind the tent had flopped forward, my father had had to pull it up so that the other father could unzip it. Inside, it was as I, too, had seen it that night, almost ready for departure. Ants everywhere, attracted by a half-eaten package of crackers. The mother gave only a glance, then sat on the grass. He shook out the sleeping bags to get rid of the ants, rolled them up. He leafed through some pages of the book that Tania was studying and put it in a bag. With my father's help he carried backpacks and all the rest to the Renault 4. Last he folded up the tent. A moment of faintness when he opened the car of his youth that he had handed down to his daughters. They'd hung a yellow doll on the rearview mirror.

He went back to his wife, who was sitting on the grass listening to the birds. I'm done, let's go, he said. Another car drove them to the hotel, in the town. After a few days the Renault 4 disappeared from Dente del Lupo, someone drove it home, to Bomporto.

They stayed a little longer, and returned for the start of the trial.

From the hospital in Teramo the rumor, starting with a nurse, passed from mouth to mouth to us: during her shift, Signora Vignati had come to see Doralice. It was the only time the Sheriff withdrew and waited outside the room. The woman didn't stay long and emerged with her tears already dry. Surely she had asked about the last hours of her daughters' lives, but only she and Doralice knew what was said. So the nurse recounted, but who believed her. People thought she was someone who invented stories to make herself important. That poor mother couldn't even stand up, no way could she, who had lost two daughters, have gone and talked to the survivor.

Doralice stayed in the hospital for ten days, more to keep her sheltered from the commotion than from necessity. The

superficial wounds healed quickly, for the one in her hip fur-
ther treatment was needed. In the ward she received letters and
small gifts of every type: chocolates, stuffed animals, good-luck
pins. The Sheriff threw away the overabundance of flowers,
gave candy to the nurses, and put the rest in a bag to take with
her when she went home to change. Doralice didn't even see
that stuff. She never opened the mail. Someone wrote to her
every day from Sicily calling her "my heroine," he wanted to
marry her as soon as she recovered. Who could have known the
contents of the sealed pastel-colored envelopes is only one of
the minor mysteries of that period.

I knew that the Sheriff wouldn't let anyone enter the hospital room. Maybe for me she would have made an exception, but
I didn't feel ready. I was a coward, but I, too, had to recover. I
wouldn't add my letter to all the ones Doralice didn't read. I'd
go and visit her at home, later, I vowed. We'd see each other
there.

My father sometimes ran into Osvaldo, asked about her.
Always the same answer: OK.

He said it one night over the soup. "I don't think Doralice
will ever recover."

He had heard her, still lying on that cart, as the siren was
sounding, utter the name that Osvaldo had asked for earlier:
Vasile.

3

Doralice and I could say we knew him, or at least we'd seen him more than once that summer. I don't know precisely when he had arrived in Italy, illegally. Ciarango had hired him, maybe two or three years before. Someone in need, he answered if he was asked who was the foreigner. Some nights, when everything was settled in the pen, he'd take him to the Sheriff's *casotto*, for a beer. He rode Fulmine, the other followed on the mule they used for the milk cans.

Doralice and I looked at him, he seemed our contemporary. He was. He also looked at us, in silence, his eyes blue beneath the blond hair. He held the cold bottle in his hands and occasionally exchanged a few words in dialect with Ciarango, who had taught him. They were dirty in the same way, the same animal smell clung to them. Nasty rumors circulated among men, Doralice heard them in the field: the boy, too, coupled with the sheep.

There were others like him, scattered throughout the mountains, working for the shepherds. They slept in the pens and spent all their time with the flocks. Sometimes on Saturdays they cleaned up and shaved to go to the town, I'd run into them on the bus. I had also met Vasile one day; I already knew his name. I was going home and he to Dente del Lupo, he would get off at the last stop and continue on foot for a good stretch. He was sitting by himself in a seat on the aisle, two rows ahead, examining what he'd bought in a bag. Razors, I saw out of the corner of my eye, shaving cream. He felt my curiosity, pushed his things deeper inside and tied the bag.

When Doralice said his name, Osvaldo couldn't believe it. He turned to my father and waited there, in the Trignanis' farmyard, until the ambulance siren stopped.

"Vasile?" he repeated to his daughter.

He knew him better than we did, on a few occasions he had invited him for a drink at the *casotto*. Doralice confirmed it by squeezing her eyelids, and the doctor was already beside her. At those moments Osvaldo must have doubted her. Maybe she was confusing him with someone else. Vasile wasn't bad. And then the men like him all seemed the same, silent, cold-eyed.

The only one he could ask was Ciarango, who was sitting there on the ground, with his back to the barn wall. Osvaldo went over to him, his height cast a shadow.

"What's the name of the man working for you?" he asked.

The mouth moved in his beard as if he were preparing to speak, then a studied silence.

"You know his name is Vasile," he answered finally.

My father also came over. Osvaldo was in a hurry, he looked at the group moving around his daughter. They had already taken her vital signs, they were preparing to load her into the ambulance. Then he asked him pointblank.

"Did you give him the pistol?"

The other played at exasperating him with his slowness. No. He would have liked to know where that blasted kid had ended up—he hadn't seen him since the day before, and he'd taken Fulmine. Pause. And he hadn't given him anything, apart from bread and cheese. But what sort of questions were these. In the mountains everyone went around armed, to defend against wolves and wild dogs. He, Osvaldo, wasn't he the first to go into the beechwood with a gun over his shoulder?

"I said pistol, not gun."

Gun, pistol, for Ciarango it was the same. The pistol was more convenient if you had to frighten an animal, no? A lot of the shepherds had one.

Doralice was already on the stretcher, the doctor was talking to her, certainly to reassure her. The driver was ready, with a nod he invited Osvaldo to get in the ambulance. At that moment my father turned to Ciarango and said, without anger: "You were wrong, you and the others, to take these foreigners and leave them alone with your animals."

They couldn't find him, for a long time searching paths, fields, and sheepfolds. At the shelter his jacket hung on a nail in the wall. Outside the sheep wandered nervously because their breasts were full of milk and hurting. For more than twenty-four hours no one had milked them. And still Ciarango couldn't take care of them, with all those policemen rummaging everywhere among his things. At a certain point the sergeant showed the marshal something he had in his hand: bullets. Then they started to press Ciarango. But what did he have to do with it, they belonged to the worker, he said.

Obviously he wasn't telling the truth, and for days continued to deny it. He repeated even there the story of the mountain teeming with wild beasts, and of shepherds who went around armed. They, the police, should have known that.

What sort of day was it for me? I had stayed at Dente del Lupo, the news arrived in confusing, contradictory fragments. It spread in waves through the crowd of reporters and the curious. Since early morning people had been coming up from the town, some even left work in order not to miss the news while it was happening.

I was with the Sheriff when she answered the phone. Then she couldn't hang it up she was shaking so hard. She's alive, she said. She knelt under the image of her Madonna and thanked her a thousand times. The receiver came off the phone on the wall and remained hanging on the wire, swaying slightly with the voice of Osvaldo, who was calling her: Hey, Nunziati'. I leaned over her and hugged her from behind, I couldn't hold her broad shoulders, agitated by her weeping. A few moments and she recovered, she had to hurry to her daughter.

I put the receiver back. A feeling of lightness raised me from the floor. The fear accumulated on that long night dissolved all at once. Doralice was safe, my small betrayal hadn't been fatal. I would never tell her that I had been at the beach without her. After all, among friends those are things that can happen.

I, too, was safe. I could have gone to the mountains with them. She had proposed it: let's go on an outing, before the bad weather starts. What had happened to Doralice, or to the other two girls, could have happened to me.

4.

It was Fulmine who betrayed him. He wasn't an ordinary horse. A hiker had seen him at Campo Imperatore, in the afternoon light. Not too close, but close enough to notice the long scar that marked his face. Riding him was a young man with pale hair, it seemed to him, but he wasn't sure because of the sun in his eyes. It had been a moment, a wild gallop over the gilded field.

The man was taking off his boots beside the car. Then he had heard on the radio that the police were looking for a man on horseback who might know something regarding the crime at Dente del Lupo. He turned back, following the road in the direction of that gallop. So he reached the old hotel near the rope tow. It was closed, on a sign the start and end dates of works never carried out. On the ground floor there must have been a bar, through the dirty window you could see the drinks fridge with an old Coca-Cola ad. The hiker, a soldier on leave, circled the building on foot.

There were no signs of life at the back, either, only the whistle of the wind at altitude. Then a sound different from his footsteps made him jump: the horse was tied to a scaffolding, swishing its tail to chase away the flies. It offered its muzzle to be caressed. No trace of whoever had brought him there.

The man headed to the car. In front of the bar the fleeting impression of a figure moving inside. He stood still for a moment: nothing more. Maybe it had been his own reflection in the dusty glass. But the horse was real, tied to the scaffolding at the back.

The hiker reached the village of Santo Stefano, called the police. He told them about the horse, tied up alone behind the Mussolini hotel. Around here we always called it that, because Mussolini had been kept prisoner there.

In no time Marshal Capasso had organized the team, and three cars left from Dente del Lupo. They stopped before arriving, so as not to be seen. They walked the last stretch, and surrounded the hotel. Capasso directed his men with gestures, the horse wasn't in the back, but an agent noticed fresh manure in front of the window of the bar. A minute later they were inside. They continued silently through corridors and kitchens, laundry. Behind the door of the boiler room, the cops heard Fulmine breathing through his nostrils. The horse was standing nervously, and he was sitting on the floor, the reins loose in his hands. He wasn't armed, offered no resistance. They had come a long way to get there.

No one ever knew for sure what happened afterward in that room. They must have put away the guns, led the horse outside. Then some of them almost certainly lost control. By the time they came down from the hotel it was almost dark. They must have passed along the road between the campground and the Sheriff's *casotto*, under the street lights. Capasso in the first Alfetta received compliments via radio on the best day of his career.

Dozens of people had gathered, they greeted the cops with applause. In the second car the agents tried to cover him up, but everyone could see his nose was bruised, eyes swollen shut, cracked lip. Only at the trial were the two broken incisors noticed, the few times he opened his mouth. No one believed he had fallen off the horse, as was said.

The crowd wanted him for itself, his battered condition wasn't enough. Those closest tried to block the car, pounded on the windows. Accelerating rapidly, the cops got him off.

My father found me exhausted in the crowd. I was wandering

around in confusion, uncertain whether to stay. It was pointless now, and yet I couldn't drag myself away. If I moved even
a short distance, nothing was true anymore. He looked at me
curiously, as if he didn't recognize me. He, too, was different,
those two days had left him thinner, his forehead more wrin-
kled. From that point on, every moment of our lives would fall
in a before or an after, there was no need to name it: the crime.

"You can't stay here forever, now go and sleep. I'm going up
to Ciarango."

"I'll come, then go home with you."

We drove up the dirt road in silence, only every so often a
rock seemed to dent the Ritmo from below.

"I don't know how Doralice is, Osvaldo hasn't come back
from the hospital," my father said.

The coincidence of our thoughts about her struck me. I
imagined she'd be released in a few days, and then would slowly
forget. Trust in her future warmed my heart. I was twenty years
old, and it still seemed to me so easy to erase damage. That
night, under the late-August stars, was perhaps the last chance
I had to believe it.

My father wanted to tell Ciarango about the capture,
maybe he didn't know. The sheep were sleeping in the pen, by
now he must have milked them. The odor of milk was strong.
We set off toward the shelter. It hadn't rained for weeks, our
feet sank into mud we weren't expecting. My father turned
on the flashlight, he aimed it ahead of us. The ground was
wet, in various places white puddles were widening. An overturned milk can in the field, then another and another. One
was all dented, as if it had been thrown against the rock. My
father cursed, called Ciarango, shouted to him. Only the dogs
answered. The door of the shelter was wide open, and, inside,
the table, the shepherd's cot, the few chairs were turned upside
down. The flashlight pitiless in the chaos of broken bottles, and
he could be anywhere.

The strange respect my father had for that man surprised me. He risked his friendship with Osvaldo for him. What had happened to him, we wondered, coming down from the pen. And who could have wrecked the shelter. We girls had always made fun of him at the *casotto*, we held our noses behind him. He waited for summer only to get away from everyone and live in the mountains, free, with the animals. My father understood his retreat without God, maybe even sometimes envied him.

That night Ciarango didn't much matter to me. Vasile's face in the police car, just two hours earlier, kept coming back to me. Though he was disfigured by the beating you saw how young he was. I still didn't want to believe it had been him.

No one in the valley forgot his boy's face, we stopped him forever at that precise moment of his life, the moment of the photographs that appeared in the papers, beside the headline: *Monster with the face of an angel.*

5

It's not easy to talk about what happened afterward. We lost the place of our summers without even knowing it. The campground was sealed off, but it was the end of the season, and with the first rains it would have closed anyway. At the time the extent of the change escaped us.

We young people no longer climbed up to Dente del Lupo, nor did the members of the Alpine Club practice anymore on the cliff of Pietra Rotonda. Dario said he wouldn't have been able to climb up to where he'd found Tania. On the other hand, people came from the outside just to see the exact spot.

Our birthplace had protected us for a long time, or maybe that had been a false impression. We grew up in a single night.

It's not easy to talk about Doralice and me. Afterward she left the house only for the trial sessions. She didn't miss one, she was always dressed the same, in jeans and a shirt, light or woolen, according to the season. Her hair was pulled back in a ponytail that gradually got longer down her back. The Sheriff and Osvaldo came with her every day and kept the reporters away, sometimes rudely. I never had the courage to go and see her.

No one was surprised that she left school, not even her parents. In fact, they hadn't really believed in it before. They had let her enroll in the University of Chieti, but what use would the degree be. They would never have been able to buy a pharmacy, at most she would have worked as an assistant. As far as the Sheriff was concerned, she might as well look for a job as a salesperson in a store. Certainly they didn't force her to go back to her books. Later she decided on it herself, but in Canada.

Doralice was justified. And me? Nothing had happened to me. I had been stricken, like everyone, but not personally. And my friend had survived. And yet I had lost energy, my nerves were shattered, I had no willpower. I spent hours on the same two pages without memorizing them. I couldn't visualize the primary trunks of the brachial plexus in the supraclavicular region.

I didn't go back to school in October. Some classmates called me, I made excuses. Family problems, but I'd be back soon. It's a stage, my mother whispered, venting to someone on the phone. I failed the neurology exam and didn't take any others in that session. My father scolded once or twice, less than I expected. My mother kept him informed him of my state. One day she told him to leave me alone, maybe I had some kind of nervous exhaustion. I heard them.

Some mornings I'd try. Early wakeup, coffee, textbooks and notebooks ready on my desk. I copied diagrams in the hope of memorizing them. I scribbled around them and then on them, erasing them. I wrote "Lucia" here and there on the page until my name no longer meant anything. After a while I'd get sleepy. I'd rest my cheek on the anatomical charts and sleep for a while. If I repeated them aloud, walking back and forth between the door and the window, it didn't last. A detail was enough to distract me, my father starting up the tractor outside, the wind rising. Everything I studied was so meaningless. I imagine it's the same for Amanda.

I went outside, since it was pointless to persist. Around the house were fruit trees of every variety, then some withered. I looked at the leaves that that year drifted down poignantly. My father stopped the tractor and looked at me, grinding his teeth. I helped him pick persimmons, he on the ladder with the pail, me below arranging the fruit in boxes, still too bitter to eat.

"Be careful, the hornets are out," he said.

The hornets dug holes in the peel of the riper fruits and gradually consumed the pulp inside. If disturbed, they attacked. Once he had ended up in the emergency room, stung in the head.

His voice fell from above onto my back.

"What's got into you? You never liked working outside and now you're always here. Go do your own things."

I didn't have any of my own things. They all slipped out of my hands.

One morning in early winter he asked me to help him. It was time to take up the garden, by now even the late tomatoes were finished. My father felt snow arriving, he didn't know how much. It was a memorable year, because of the snow as well. Dente del Lupo remained buried until April. But that morning the December sun, though cold, was still shining.

We began pulling out the stakes that supported the now dried-up plants. They flopped on the ground, the last rotten tomatoes still attached. He turned at my "Ow," I had cut my palm on a splintered stake. He looked: it's nothing, I told him. He wanted to wrap around my hand one of the handkerchiefs he always carried in his pocket, I didn't want him to.

I went to the house to disinfect it. Through the back door I heard my mother talking to someone. I stopped with a jolt. I would never have expected to hear that voice I knew so well. A piece of their conversation, while I changed my shoes. How was Doralice? Eh, how was she. Always with the light on at night. If you approach her she jumps.

"But at least with you does she let it out, tell you how it happened?"

Very little. She had been shot right away and had fallen. So many things she didn't know. Maybe afterward someone else had come, but she wasn't sure. A policeman had said that.

I held my breath as I listened to the Sheriff. For the first time, amid all the gossip that proliferated that fall, I was close to the truth. A few meters from Doralice shouts, other shots, the horse's whinnying.

She had been lucky, said the Sheriff. Lucky why, my mother asked.

"That demon didn't choose her, he wanted to get Virginia."

If Doralice had been the chosen one, she wouldn't have returned.

I dragged my clogs, the sound distracted them. They were interested in my hand, it's only a scratch, I said. I disinfected it, and we were silent. Doralice's presence was so solid I could almost touch her, hear her breath and smell the sweetish perfume she'd been using. I didn't ask about her.

The Sheriff smoothed her hair with a habitual gesture. I noticed only then how white it had become in the past months and how she had aged. The deep furrows at the sides of her mouth, the double chin hanging. She asked what I was doing, apart from helping my father in the garden. Nothing, in that period. A glance between my mother and her, they had also talked about me, sitting at that bare table. She looked straight at me, severe. What was I waiting for, someone who would marry me and support me? Like the women of other times? I was the one who always wanted to make a revolution.

6.

Doralice saw death that day but didn't recognize it. She didn't know it was the young man on horseback, stopping in the woods. He was wearing a hat, maybe he'd got it at the shooting gallery at the town fair, and you couldn't see his eyes. At the trial the defense lawyer would say that he had never been to one of those fairs, and someone had given him the leather cap. Like the backpack hanging on the saddle. Nothing was his.

Doralice looked at him without suspicion, from closer up he was Vasile, the foreigner who worked for Ciarango. It was a while since they'd gone down together to have a beer at the *casotto*. She was surprised she hadn't heard him arriving. Or maybe he was already there, waiting for them, when she and her friends took the wrong path.

They had gone up around eleven, taking advantage of the sky's clearing. Tania had wanted to rest, the last day. In the tent everything was ready for their departure. The next morning the long trip home in the Renault 4. But then Doralice had stopped to say goodbye, and they hadn't wanted to waste the good weather. They could go out for a short hike.

Virginia carried only a bum bag fastened loosely around her waist. Water they would find on the way. They came to a fork in the path, and Doralice, with the assurance of one who knows the terrain, had chosen the wrong direction. They were lost. The Alpine Club's paint marks on trunks and rocks had disappeared, the sky darkened again above the tangle of branches, and some isolated drops fell.

Doralice had gone up to the young man, I'm Osvaldo's daughter, she said, not sure that he'd recognized her. She asked if there was a shortcut to get to the shelter, they would take cover there. He stared at her from above, his cheeks bristly, the color of his eyes hidden between thick lashes. He lengthened his gaze toward Virginia, who had remained slightly behind. The rumble of thunder muffled the bells of the grazing animals.

Vasile motioned with his hand toward the ridge. He tugged on the reins to move aside and let them pass. Then he followed them, slowly, on horseback. In a broken Italian he said it was dangerous for them there, because of the dogs.

What dogs, Doralice asked, she didn't know anything about dogs.

Wild dogs wandered through the woods, they mated with wolves, he explained with gestures and some words. They kept going up by the shortcut he'd indicated.

He was following along with them, covering their backs. He was quiet but polite, as death at times appears. At a certain point Doralice missed the sound of the hooves on the ground and turned. There was no longer anyone behind.

"We found him in front of us, barring the way," she said in court, responding to the defense.

Was she really sure it was the same person, the lawyer pressed her. How was it possible that one moment he was behind them and the next in front? Maybe she had the sun in her eyes and hadn't seen clearly. There was no sun, it was starting to rain, Doralice responded sharply.

Announced in the newspapers and on television, the trial began three months after the arrest. There had never been such a throng in Teramo as at those first hearings: the curious, reporters, photographers who tried to get a picture of her, the survivor, and of the murderer with the eyes of ice, as they called him. They also pursued the prosecutor, who arrived in a hurry, in a red suit and with a briefcase full of documents. Grimaldi cut through the crowd without making any statements. "The Court will decide" was the most she would say.

She had already questioned Doralice in the hospital, sitting beside the bed, speaking informally to a girl the same age as her daughter. In the courtroom she spoke firmly and clearly from the Public Prosecutor's bench. I admired her, at the one session I went to.

"Signorina, can you describe the subject?"

Doralice in the witness chair, back straight, a little rigid before the microphone. She listed height—more or less, she added—color of eyes and hair, thin lips, sharp nose. Meanwhile with her thumb and index finger she was tearing the skin around the nails of her other hand, her usual tic. Stop it, I would have liked to whisper to her, it's going to start bleeding.

"Do you see the person you've described in this court-room?" Grimaldi asked her.

Doralice turned, her neck wooden. She looked at him, sitting in his place, the accused's bench.

"It's him," she said resolutely.

For the little I could see him, Vasile remained impassive, as if he hadn't even heard her, as if nothing about her mattered to him, or about the clamoring spectators, or about life imprisonment, which at that moment was perhaps his entire future.

The defense wasn't appointed by the court, Ciarango was paying for him, so it was rumored. He had tried to reform, in those months. He spoke of himself as of a benefactor. He had welcomed the youth, who was wandering around by himself. At the time few foreigners were seen with the sheep. Who could have imagined what he would do? He had offered him work, shelter. He repeated it at the hearing, as a witness.

"And did you also give him a weapon?" Grimaldi interrupted him, sharply.

God forbid, he answered. The pistol had been at the hut

forever and he had no idea who it belonged to. Sometimes the shepherds practiced target shooting. He, Ciarango, didn't even know that Vasile had taken it.

That pistol had been found a few days before the trial started. Buried near the pen, where wild spinach grew in the sheep manure. Vasile had tried to hide it there, before taking off with Fulmine.

After the only session I attended I would have liked to go up to Doralice, hug her just for a moment. From my place I could see she'd grown thinner, her face drained of light, and the ponytail cinched with a rubber band at her neck, to get the annoyance of her hair out of the way. She'd always liked to have her hair loose and flowing, wearing curlers to make it wavy. I wanted to go up to her and was afraid.

Two or three times, when it seemed to me that she was looking toward me, I tried to raise a hand in greeting, but I don't know if she saw me. Maybe I should have raised it higher, waved it a little.

7

Some of the shepherds were called as witnesses. The bailiff appeared at their doors to deliver the summons; their wives were frightened. Peppe, Biagino, Cicione passed the word. What did they have to do with that trial? They'd done nothing, they knew nothing. They were scattered here and there with the sheep when the murders took place, but all far from Pietra Rotonda. If they made a mistake speaking in front of the judge they could get in trouble, naming someone could provoke animosity. Cicione went down to the doctor in the town and asked for a certificate. He had shingles, he said, and couldn't move. No, he couldn't show him the outbreak because it was in his lower regions and he was embarrassed. Biagino had an attack of sciatica and Peppe a high fever.

"I'm not afraid of the law," Achille said to my father.

He was the only one who showed up. He was young then, his hip intact. His flock grazed peacefully and he had no need to protest to defend the fields. He surprised everyone by answering in correct Italian, although the cadence was that of our dialect. Achille read during the long days in the open and also carried a notebook and pencil in his jacket pocket. He writes poetry, said the other shepherds, as if it were an eccentricity.

Grimaldi asked if he knew the accused. He knew him, of course. But only by sight? Not only, in the mountains he'd run into him now and then and stop to chat while the sheep were grazing. And what impression did he make?

"At first he seemed like a placid kid, though he didn't say much."

But that was normal for someone who didn't know the language, he added. He had come to Abruzzo in search of a cousin who was working for some shepherds near L'Aquila, but hadn't managed to track him down.

"In a sense Ciarango saved him, but afterward it went the way it did."

He looked at Vasile, shaking his head slightly. Not even a glance in return.

"Do you know that there has always been a pistol at the shelter?"

He didn't know. He, too, had used that shelter, some time ago, and hadn't seen any pistol.

"Do you know if Ciarango gave it to the accused?"

I object, Your Honor, the voice was raised from the defense table. According to the lawyer Grimaldi was trying to influence the witness. Objection denied, but anyway Achille didn't know.

"He did like playing with weapons a little too much."

"And how do you know that?"

In the cold months Ciarango, like everyone else, brought the sheep down to the valley. In the barn there was no need for Vasile. He remained unemployed for weeks, and he, Achille, hired him for some jobs. They went to cut wood for the following winter. During the breaks they'd have a sandwich and the boy went off. Once Achille had heard some shots and found him shooting with a pistol, in fact. But at whom, Grimaldi asked him.

"At a squirrel."

A squirrel? The prosecutor brushed the hair off her face, incredulous. A squirrel, yes. But why? Just for fun—for kicks. He didn't really want to kill it, only frighten it as it ran up and down the trunks. He was amused. But in the end he killed it, whether by accident or on purpose. A hum of disapproval ran through the public and also the members of the jury.

A kid that age, and Achille motioned toward Vasile with his chin, shouldn't have a real gun.

There were five or six sessions, I recall, no more. I knew the dates, and someone who was present brought me news. I asked for it, actually. Everyone was in a hurry to get to the end. There was a lucid and precise witness, the survivor. There was the guilty man. We were waiting only for the sentencing, for him to receive the maximum punishment.

In April Grimaldi went to Ischia for three days, but didn't escape the reporters. Two girls brutally murdered, a family destroyed, and she took a vacation on the island, with the trial still on. What a nerve, they wrote.

After the verdict, she gave a single interview, in a national daily. She said of Vasile that he had never looked her in the eye when she questioned him. If he responded at all, it was mostly in monosyllables. Even the verdict had arrived without touching him. Besides, perhaps he was better off in prison, he was clean and healthy.

"You asked for and obtained a sentence of life in prison, is it the first time you've done that?"

No. But for the first time one of the injured parties was alive, present in the courtroom, cooperating.

And you, the prosecutor, were satisfied with the objective gained?

"One can't be happy when you have a kid of twenty who will spend the rest of his life in prison. But it's the only justice we could give the victims and their families."

And what had driven a young man to commit a crime so atrocious, the reporter asked.

Who could say. The defense had appealed to the fact that he came from a difficult family, but she, Grimaldi, didn't consider that decisive. Or at least a poor upbringing wasn't all.

Then what else?

"Isolation, I think. He lived symbiotically with the sheep, he was present when they were bred. He saw three pretty girls, he wanted one."

On the page next to that part of the interview was a photo of Tania and Virginia sitting on the grass, in shorts, legs tanned. Virginia had her arms around her knees, Tania was laughing and pointing to the person taking the picture. In the background I could make out the Sheriff's *casotto*, but just a corner.

The camera roll with that photo on it was in the tent, in the baggage ready for departure, and was developed after the sisters' deaths. On it was their vacation, the places they'd been. They never saw themselves posing on Monte Coppe, along the stretch of river they'd followed, or the night of the fair in Arsita. Their parents saw them, still so alive on the Kodak paper, saw them dancing in the square, barefoot and happy to be there.

From the slightly crooked framing I could tell it was Doralice's shot, sometimes she'd even leave a finger on the edge. Now I was sure, Tania was pointing toward her on the page of the newspaper I'd bought. I read it right away, on the bench near the newsstand.

No place is safe, said Grimaldi. "Wherever man goes, he can bring evil."

She didn't share all the rhetoric about the mountain; the woods were evocative but also full of shadows. They could betray you, you could go astray. The young man had strayed from the border of the human.

"Nature is beautiful for the wealthy, not for those who have to work like slaves."

I'd never thought about it, that phrase shook me. Over time I understood that it was valid not only for the shepherd-servant. Ciarango, Osvaldo, my father: none had chosen to live in the valley. They had stayed in the only place possible, where they were born. They hadn't seen anything else, or imagined it. They were slaves of a necessity. It affected my mother, too, and me.

The beauty surrounding us didn't concern us. We didn't

admire nature, we had to fight it. A storm that hit the ripe grain was enough to make us a little poorer. We fought against the wind, the illnesses of the animals, and the parasites on the plants. The nature that nourished us was the same that starved us. When we left the valley we didn't know how to behave in the world.

How did the survivor save herself, the reporter asked Grimaldi.

"With all her strength she wanted to live. He had to silence her at all costs, of the three she was the only one who knew him. He searched for her for hours, day and night, and a few times he came very close, we found the traces. Her instinct for self-preservation saved her."

Instinct for self-preservation, Grimaldi said. Maybe the same that later led Doralice so far away from here, and forever. And maybe also what brought Amanda back.

8.

My mother had never traveled and she felt more secure with me. She got the idea suddenly, and asked me to go with her to visit her cousin, who had been inviting her to Naples for years. At first I said no, at that time I said no to everything. But then I had never been to Naples, I could go around on my own while she was with her cousin.

On Sundays the bus was almost empty, my mother sat next to me. At six in the morning the smell of cheese from the bag she had at her feet was nauseating. I had told her not to take it, but we couldn't show up without a gift. Despite its many wrappings, it stank. My father had driven us to Pescara with a doubtful expression and returned immediately. She reminded him to water the geraniums and he: Right, I'm thinking about geraniums, with all that alfalfa to harvest. I can only imagine how it must have worried her to leave him alone at haying time, but she wanted to take me away for a few days.

On the bus I stared out at the countryside, otherwise she would have been chatting about something that didn't interest me. My mother was afraid of silence.

The night before I had come home past midnight, after one of those endless meetings at the Alpine Club office. There, too, people were talking about the trial, that was why I went. Dario had already been questioned about finding Tania's body. His friends wanted to know how it had gone, then they made plans for hikes, and ended by having a drink.

He had driven me home, and it got late in his car. We had also fallen asleep for a little afterward.

I pointed out to my mother the Maiella, with snow still on the peak. The sacred mountain, scattered with monasteries. It had a gentle, unthreatening shape. In the valley we could no longer look at our mountains, they had become so dark. Corno Grande, Prena, Tremoggia loomed over us. Dente del Lupo wasn't even mentioned anymore. Many people called for the death penalty for Vasile: if it didn't exist it should be restored for him. According to some, Ciarango, who had hired him, and given him the gun, should also be in prison. The old women prayed for the innocent souls of Tania and Virginia. My mother was taking me away from all those voices. She must have been truly worried about me, more than I thought.

Her cousin came to get us at the bus station, hot and sweaty, happy to have us in Naples. She hadn't seen me for several years, said she found me grown up and pretty, but I didn't believe her. She plunged boldly into the traffic and extended the journey slightly to show us the seaside, Castel dell'Ovo, Vesuvio from a distance. My mother held onto the door handle and stiffened as Anna hazardously passed other cars. My mother was nearly robbed when we were stopped in a traffic jam. A boy aimed at her bracelet, Anna closed the window just in time. His palm remained stamped for a moment on the glass.

"Take off whatever jewelry you have on, we're not in Abruzzo here," Anna said, tires screeching as she started up.

She lived in a sixth-floor apartment at Fuorigrotta, with her husband and mother-in-law. They were too close to the stadium, which she pointed out to us in passing, and on alternate Sundays they ended up in the chaos of the match.

At lunch the pecorino had its moment of glory as an antipasto, they cut it in half. The last time she went back she had gotten some at the Sheriff's, Anna recalled. A pause and then: "The daughter barely escaped, eh."

They had followed the trial on television.

"It could have happened to her, too, I shudder just to think of it," my mother said.

Head down, I felt everyone looking at me. Anna's mother-in-law got up with an effort, opened the window. We needed air. During the entire visit she called me *piccere'*, little one. From the room of her grandchildren, who now lived elsewhere, I heard her snoring loudly at night, but it was more the silence of her pauses that kept me awake. Around me were posters of Maradona in the blue shirt with the number 10, above the bed hung Naples team banners and flags, almost phosphorescent in the darkness.

On Monday Anna had to work, she listed the numbers of the buses going in various directions, and wished us a fun day. It wasn't easy to have fun with my mother. She refused to take the metro, being underground scared her. She didn't know how to stroll, she always walked quickly, as if she were escaping something. We had enough money, but she didn't want to buy anything, not even at the Antignano market. In order not to look at the clothes, she became spellbound before the fish stalls, and the enormous octopuses. Choose something for yourself, what I have is enough for me, she said.

I hated her spirit of sacrifice. I didn't want to be like her. I would have taken everything I could, I would enjoy youth and the rest. But, after all, it didn't go that way. My mother marked me more than I thought at twenty, I ended up too much like her.

Only walking around the *Veiled Christ* did she stop, meditating for a moment before that face. It's incredible, she said on the way out, it's really a veil, but stone.

Where are you taking me today, she asked in the morning at breakfast. Along the sea in Naples in May it was summer. Women had taken off their stockings, some were already tanned. I observed my mother's legs, as she ate *pizza a portafoglio*: the thick black hairs crushed by flesh-colored stockings. I was embarrassed for her.

That night I talked secretly with Anna, and after dinner she heated wax in a pan. She sent husband and mother-in-law to bed, we went into the bathroom. My mother cried out at every tug, but she was also laughing. It didn't seem true that the hairs imprisoned in the sticky strips were all hers. At the end she caressed the smooth skin, she couldn't stop looking at herself. If your father sees me, she said. But it was the thought of a moment, he and his bales of hay were so far from us.

"Now we'll move on to the nails," Anna said.

She filed, cut bits of skin from those hands much older than my mother's forty years. My mother continued to rebel weakly, but by now it was almost for show. No one had ever cared for her body, not even when she got married. Nail polish no, she protested, but Anna was already brushing it on, a lovely shade of red.

For a few minutes, without saying so, we were happy, during that week. I forgot the books I couldn't study, the ongoing trial, Doralice. I can see my mother again, sitting one morning at a table in a café. She had turned her chair toward the sea and stretched out her bare legs. She closed her eyes. From so far away the valley was a tiny place in the shadows.

She brought home a skirt she bought at the last minute, in Via dei Tribunali. She would wear it for a communion, in June. She called it the little skirt, as if to diminish that daring gesture of vanity.

I slept most of the way home on the bus. When we reached Pescara, in the late afternoon, I saw what she had done. She hadn't taken up the crochet work of the journey to Naples, no. She had scraped off the nail polish, removing every trace of color. All that remained were the scratches of nails on nails.

9.

The trial ended in June of 1994, less than two years after the crime. I remember those days, I was about to graduate. I was rereading my thesis, on malocclusions and posture, while I followed on TV the closing arguments of the prosecution and the defense. Grimaldi didn't have to work too hard, she simply reviewed her work: the testimony of the principal witness was completely credible; the accused was competent to stand trial, as the expert's report verified.

"This man intended to kill," the prosecutor said, referring to Tania's and Virginia's lungs, pierced by bullets. The word "man" seemed out of proportion for a face that still bore traces of adolescence.

Grimaldi lingered on his coldness, on the indifference shown toward the victims.

"He wanted one of them, he shot the two who were in his way."

At the preliminary hearing he had confessed. But the first shot had gone off by mistake and one of them had thrown a rock at him, then he had lost control. He denied the rape: that girl had undressed by herself.

Undressed by herself, the prosecutor repeated in her summation. She was silent for a moment, and during that pause she stared at the judge and then, one by one, at the women of the jury.

Later in the course of the trial the accused had said that the confession was extorted with threats: he and the three girls hadn't met that morning in August, Doralice was confused.

"The witness never had a moment's uncertainty, despite the trauma she suffered," and Grimaldi turned toward her.

Those who were close enough could see Doralice motionless in her seat, her face pinched, the ponytail longer and longer down her back. She had reached the end of the trial without a single absence.

In the last part of the closing argument, replayed by all the TV stations, Grimaldi, in robe and bib, spoke about Doralice. She thanked her for her testimony, which had allowed a fair trial to unfold. She admired the courage she had shown in re-living every moment in the presence of the accused, the Court, and the public.

"And now, ladies and gentlemen, it's up to us. It's up to us to offer her solace, if only in part, for what she suffered. We have to respond to her demand for justice."

With her arm outstretched and palm open first in the direction of the judge, then toward the jurors, she concluded: "How could we disappoint her? Who of us would carry on our conscience the weight of a defeat of the truth?"

Beside Doralice the Sheriff was weeping; for a moment, in a single frame you could see her whole body, shaken by sobs. Osvaldo's hand on her shoulder.

The defense lawyer wasn't the same as before. The big name did not show up for the final contest, and his associate seemed uneasy. The half confessions later retracted by his client caught him off guard. This was a youth of twenty-one, he said, who had been left to himself; he had no bond with his family of origin, and here not even a friend. His only contact was with animals, day and night, and that brutalized him.

"Even if on Saturday you can go to town, where do you introduce yourself?"

At that age he still needed a guide, and Ciarango wasn't a guide, he was only a master. Even if he was competent to stand trial, said the lawyer, Vasile Hirdo was nevertheless an immature youth, in terms of both age and experience. He hadn't been able to control his instincts and a weapon in his backpack hadn't helped.

The robe slid over one shoulder, exposing the polka dots of his shirt. The sentence would have been the same for Vasile, but the lawyer, apart from his inexperience, hadn't believed in him firmly enough.

"Life in prison" fell into the perfect silence of the courtroom. Solitary confinement for a year and the other accessory penalties that the judge announced right afterward didn't diminish the cold echo of the words. Anyway, Vasile wouldn't be able to pay the expenses of the trial. Above all he would never be able to pay the Vignati and Damiani families compensation for the damage he had done.

He listened to the sentence standing, without moving a muscle. The interpreter, who had been close to him during the hearings, remained mute, like the lawyer.

Tears fell from beneath the dark glasses that Tania and Virginia's father wore, their mother was stone. A murmuring among the public, somewhere at the back of the courtroom isolated applause.

The crowd of reporters outside was uncontainable. They thronged toward Doralice. Signorina Damiani, a statement after the sentencing. Are you satisfied? She stared at a point in front of her. Osvaldo and the Sheriff stood firm in the middle, hands raised against cameras and flashes.

It was the last time. Reporters and photographers left their stations, ate crepes in broth again in the restaurants. Then cars and vans left, the hotels of Teramo emptied. By the next day the city had become boring again.

In the town I expected there'd be a lot of talk. There wasn't. Everyone knew and was silent. Suddenly we lost the sense of importance that the furor around the trial had given us. That name, Dente del Lupo, forever associated with the crime. Shame descended on us.

Two weeks later I graduated. I don't know exactly what had driven me to return to my books. But what could I do. It wasn't the return of willpower, as my mother thought. Rather, I didn't want to end up like her. All that labor in the fields and not a penny. The first money of her own she got from was tiny pension.

Vasile remained in the prison of Marino del Tronto for seven years. Only Ciarango went to see him, but not long afterward he died. After the period of solitary confinement the guards were still supposed to protect Vasile from the other prisoners, but they didn't always manage to stop the beatings.

When he was extradited the press reported the news, and the case was discussed again. "You'll see that where he's from they'll let him out," said my father.

The parents of the victims wouldn't comment. They never came to Abruzzo again, not even on the anniversary of the deaths of Tania and Virginia. At the base of Pietra Rotonda a ceramic photo recalls them to passersby, they smile forever in their unfinished youth.

Doralice has lived in Canada for years now. She's a lawyer, her mother says. She comes back as seldom as she can. To all the questions that I didn't ask she responded with a long letter, at the start of her life there. I keep it among my papers; it's lasted through all my moves.

She had survived, and I, too, had survived. The shadow that engulfed her, and touched me, had left us in silence. But that letter was necessary, for me and for her.

Here's Doralice: on paper, too, that scratchy voice she had at the trial. She had crossed the ocean for me.

Hey, Lucia, she began like that. She no longer sat on the side of the accuser, she had put herself in the seat of the accused.

If I hadn't gone over to say goodbye to them that day at the campground nothing would have happened. They wouldn't have left the tent. Then I also took the wrong path and when I saw him

*I asked about a shortcut to the shelter. How lucky to meet him, I
thought. It was starting to rain, Tania and Virginia were getting
alarmed. He was looking at us insistently, especially at Virginia's
legs, and breasts, but at the moment I didn't pay attention to that.
He was polite, he came with us. At a narrow point he blocked the
path with the horse, got down. You know Fulmine, Ciarango's
horse. We didn't understand his words, so with gestures he told
Virginia to get undressed. Then I made my biggest mistake. I
should have yelled: let's go! We could still save ourselves, run
away, go down where we'd come from. Instead I asked him if he'd
gone crazy. I threatened to tell my father, and Ciarango. They'll
rip you to pieces, I said. Coldly, he opened the backpack hanging
on the horse's saddle. He shot me right away, I fell on the ground,
maybe more out of fear. They were crying, begging him. I was in
shock but I heard: Virginia offered him the little money she had
in her pack. Another shot, for Tania. And I decided to be dead.
His footsteps came closer, his shoe on my hip. He pressed to see
if I would react. I didn't. I wasn't even breathing. My heart, my
blood was all stopped. I didn't know if I was pretending or if I
was really dead. I opened my eyes for an instant. He was on top
of Virginia, she was screaming, but more and more softly. Her
sister's cries had already stopped.*

*I started creeping toward the thick part of the woods. As long
as I heard him panting I was sure he wasn't thinking of me. I got
up, for a few seconds I saw black. Then I started running. Behind
me the last shots. He followed me, sometimes he got close and I
hid. I crouched under the Scaglia, the dirt he moved with his feet
fell in front of my face. He had to find me at all costs, and there
were moments I was so tired I almost wanted to give in. Finally I
realized he'd lost me, but I was also losing my strength. I was still
bleeding a little. I went down, blindly in the wind. It got dark
and I didn't know where I was, not in my head, either. But I felt
that they were looking for me. I got to the scree by chance, the
stones carried me rolling down.*

Lucky you didn't come that day.

She wrote about herself and me, about Tania and Virginia, whom she hadn't been able to protect. She wrote to tell me that she had escaped while he was raping Virginia.

Every night I hear her voice.

THE CONCERT

1.

T he Sheriff doesn't know what put it in his mind. And at
his age. These are not the years for big projects. Time is
limited, energy fades. He should think about maintain-
ing the health he still has.

"We can plant a garden, a small one, raise a few chickens.
We can't reopen the conversation about the mountain. But
Osvaldo is stubborn, he won't listen to me."

She came here to tell me this. She left the Ape in the farmyard. She gripped the banister going up the stairs. Her body
burdens her. We're sitting on the terrace at my father's house.
We watch him from above, as he scrambles alongside the combine that's just arrived. The big machine looms over him, he has
to shout to make himself heard by the man driving. Start there,
he says, and points angrily at the field where he wants him to
go first.

The Sheriff shakes her head slowly.

"He's like Osvaldo, they haven't learned much from life.
Look at your father, half crippled he still wants to run."

He sees her, raises his arm to wave. If he'd heard her, he
would have shouted an insult.

The combine cuts the wheat, swallows it. It accumulates
the grains in the shoe, spits the straw out on the dry earth. My
father makes sure that nothing is wasted. The Sheriff speaks
louder, above the whining noise.

"I heard about your daughter, that she was at the demon-
stration. I didn't expect it."

174 · DONATELLA DI PIETRANTONIO

I, too, discovered it when I saw her, I say. But there were so many kids, they're against Gerí's plans for Dente del Lupo.

"I know that man, he's a profiteer."

On the TV news the Sheriff has seen young people protesting to save the planet. But at Dente del Lupo that's not the only issue. You can't build in a place like that. It should be left in peace.

"You know how many times we tried to meet the parents, after the crime. Also at the trial. They would never listen to us. But it wasn't our fault, we, too, paid dearly."

Doralice called yesterday. You could hear her so clearly, she seemed very close. She won't come back for her vacation this year, either: maybe at Christmas. A daughter who lives on the other side of the ocean is lost. In another way, but she's lost. No phone call can bring her back to you from seven thousand kilometers away. Sometimes speaking with her father she doesn't remember how to say something in dialect, English slips out. The Sheriff's voice loses its composure, breaks.

They've never gone to visit her. They aren't capable of it. Just seeing airplanes in the sky scares her. She points to a distant contrail, which is fading, vaporous, into the blue. And then the airport, amid all those people—she breaks out in a sweat just thinking about it. She rests her large, round arms, covered with mosquito bites, on the plastic tablecloth. She has sweet blood, she says, catching my look.

A sudden desire to hug her, and be hugged by her. Like that night at the campground, in anguish for Doralice. I don't move.

"Don't fight with Amanda, it's not worth the money Gerí's offering."

And it's not worth it for that place, she adds, looking up toward the mountain. You have to have patience with her, she's twenty. "Leave her alone, if she's not studying now."

"How did you know?" I ask.

My father told her, once when he went to see them. He was worried.

"The road is somewhere, but your daughter still has to find it."

I listen to her words in silence, with a sense of gratitude. If my mother were here now, she would say almost the same thing. She would say: Wait. Maybe it's really she who is speaking to me through Nunziatina. After all, they were friends. And if my mother had something to forgive her for, I'm sure that in life she must have done so.

"If you have to go against my husband, as far as I'm concerned you can do it. That's what I came to tell you."

2.

My heart is pounding as I unlock the gate with my key. It's morning, and still cool here. As usual the gate is resistant against the ground, I force it until it opens. The excavator follows me, stops in front of the small one-story structure. The man gets out and looks around: we want to start from here, he asks? It was the reception area, and the Sheriff's office. All right, I say. He gets back in and starts the engine, the demolishing bucket approaches the roof, a little timid, tastes the edge of it. Then it moves decisively, bites and retreats, throws the pieces into the back of a truck that's just arrived. I'm spellbound, as when I was a child staring at the rotations of a cement mixer. But that's the sort of thing boys like, my mother protested.

Amanda took care of the estimates. She got in touch with the companies and brought a couple up here, to inspect. I didn't think demolition would cost so much. What did you expect, my father said. He wanted to contribute something, but Osvaldo absolutely shouldn't know.

"You and your daughter will end up making me fight with him."

But deep down he seems content with my decision.

The bucket proceeds, crunches the façade as if it were a cookie. It arrives at the faded drawing of the wolf, bites its head and reduces it to rubble. It consumes the memory of Doralice who painted the fur with a brush, balancing on the top step of a ladder. That muzzle, I said to her, looking at it from a few meters away. And she, turning: what's wrong with that muzzle. It seems like a fox's. So I'll round it a little.

The bucket consumes the dreams Osvaldo had when he built these walls. I gave him a few thousand euros, as a compensation not owed. There's nothing here that's worth anything. He twisted his head slightly and folded the check in two, put it in the back pocket of his pants. We'd met again near the landslide, but this time he didn't invite me to his house. He turned the Ape around and went off immediately.

Days pass, I didn't imagine it would take all this time. Clear and overcast skies alternate, clouds of every shape. Some afternoons it rains, men and machines stop. In the shelter of an awning I open the thermos, offer coffee already sugared. The air turns cold.

I took some vacation. I'm always here, following the work, I don't even know why. Every so often Amanda joins me, and stays awhile. She asked a worker if the waste materials are being disposed of properly. Of course, signorina, he answered, it's the law.

On the back of the toilets the red phrases fell along with the wall, letter by letter. KILL HIM became L HIM then M. Virginia and Tania's names disappeared first, and right afterward the other line, that wanted them alive forever.

The pool was left. The excavator traveled around it, removing the earth. As the walls were exposed, they were demolished. On the bottom the workers used a pneumatic drill, headphones over their ears. I listened, my mind blank, to the sound as it echoed, amplified, off the rocks. I was gripped only by a sense of ending, and of completion.

Yesterday my father came to see. Under his eyes a last load of rubble and pipes departed. The hole, looked at from the edge, seemed to us enormous.

"This is the biggest crazy thing Osvaldo did," he admitted.

"But you always protected him," I said.

"For a friend you do that, and even worse. Sometimes you do things you wouldn't do for a child."

Amanda also showed up: Hey, Grandpa, she greeted him. And to me: "If the company brings us the dirt, we can fill it ourselves, here."

"You who?" my father was surprised.

"She and I, so we'll save a little."

A laugh escaped him. You and she. Here it's not like giving a massage or writing with a pen. I'd like to see you, with your soft little hands. I'm coming tomorrow, for sure.

And tomorrow is already today.

The workers are going to load the dirt from a road construction site nearby, they've already thrown a little in the hole. Then we'll take care of it, as Amanda wanted. She told some of the kids from the Alpine Club, they've come to help us. We're six or seven, with shovels, hoes, and spades. She's among those at the bottom, sweaty, hair pulled back, legs dirty sticking out from the shorts. They level, trample hard to firm the ground that will come. I throw the earth from above. Tonight the blisters that are already forming on our hands will burst, they'll hurt.

"But look at your daughter, she seems to have suddenly woken up." My father is amazed.

I nod. I hope but don't trust, Amanda lives by moments. Then she retreats to something she doesn't know or doesn't say.

He observes, curious. Then he can't restrain himself, he approaches the edge: and don't they see those two empty corners? Fill in there, he shouts, not just in the middle. He waves to point out where. The kids stop, listen to him dumbstruck. They obey. They're clumsy, but they're repairing the damage to the meadow and perhaps, after thirty years, the wound we still carry inside.

At one o'clock I hand out sandwiches, they devour them in two minutes. I'm afraid there won't be enough, you get hungrier in the mountains.

We're almost finished. The surface just has to be compacted slightly. Now my father intervenes in person, he stamps his feet and the shovel in a kind of comic ballet. *Dang dang*. Where the reflections of sky and woods trembled on the water, where I swam among the tourists under Doralice's gaze, this black and virgin earth now lies.

3.

Amanda left a week ago, and I can't get used to her absence. Yesterday I bought her rice milk, but she won't drink it. We parted in an argument, she already had her backpack over her shoulders, and we hadn't finished saying what we wanted to say. She told me almost at the last minute, as usual. Rather, it was me asking her if she intended to go back to the university, now that it's September. But no, she was going away. That's how I found out.

How far our children's thoughts are sometimes from what we imagine them. That false consonance with them is only a memory of their infancy.

Going back to school really doesn't interest her. Continuing with the course she'd chosen doesn't interest her, and, besides, her credits don't even add up to twenty. She confessed it, without shame. Her father and I are fixated on a degree. She looked at me with a sense of superiority, maybe some contempt.

I rose in this little world, left the land and now live in the town. I have a clinic in the center. What has value for me hardly counts at all for my daughter. Work, with which we fill our lives. My small position, her father's banking career. Nothing that she would consider. A degree will not decide who she is.

She left for a month, the period of the grape harvest. Now she's there, picking bunches of Verdicchio on the hills of Jesi. With all the grapes there are to pick in Abruzzo. She'll earn the minimum she needs for fall and winter, she said. She doesn't know the cost of life.

Maybe in the meantime she'll change her mind. The work in the fierce sun, the sticky juice that drips along your arms and, mixed with sweat, attracts wasps. Or maybe only we from the countryside still believe that manual labor makes you appreciate studying.

This time of year, when she went to school, we bought textbooks, I enrolled her in swimming and rhythmic gymnastics. Today I can't make any decisions for her, she reminded me before leaving.

For some reason as I listened to her my thoughts went back to that night in Milan when she was wounded, alone on the street. Very belatedly I apologized. I'm sorry I didn't come the next day, I still can't explain it to myself. She was silent for a few seconds. It wouldn't have changed anything, she said. But I can't forgive myself. There are moments when you have to enter the life of your child, even if it seems pointless.

Amanda took a bag, already packed, from her room, carried it to the door. I shouldn't worry. She put her arms through the straps of the backpack, settled it on her shoulders. She met my gaze as far as the door, then she turned and left.

Her resolution impressed me. Reality will break off those sharp edges.

That night she sent me a message. She had arrived, she would sleep with the others in a big farmhouse amid the vineyards. A smiling emoji and a bunch of grapes. Good night, I wrote her later.

Days ago I confided to Rubina that today I might lack the courage to have children. I was talking like that only because I was angry, she said.

I sent her father an email. He called soon afterward, worried. I couldn't talk at that moment: call me later, I said.

She can't waste any more time, Dario was angry. The years pass, others get ahead, have jobs. I recognized the anxiety in his breath. He doesn't understand that Amanda won't take that route. How different children are, seen from a distance. Blurry, imprecise. Unreal.

He was so upset that I didn't want to tell him. I made an appointment with a lawyer, for the separation. I'll write to him one of these days, and he'll agree.

He says he'll go talk to Amanda in the vineyards, try to persuade her. Then I, too, get attached to that faint hope. Like him I can't resign myself. I can't accept that my daughter will achieve less than me. Her renunciation is my failure.

For now she's there. For a month I'm free of responsibility: a relief. I'm free of her. I think that and am immediately ashamed. A wave of affection submerges me. I see her amid the vines, hair always escaping from the tie that holds it back. She worries me, I love her. More than anything I love her. It will be a long September.

4

The days are shorter and at night it's already autumn here. I sent a message to the group warning them to cover up. I arrived early, like a lady of the house preparing to receive guests. But I had nothing to do, not even open the gate that's no longer there. The Sheriff's *casotto* has disappeared, across the road. The enclosure, the structures, and the pool are gone. The field was ready on its own, empty at the edge of the woods. There are traces of the recent work of the excavator: where it bit, where it flattened.

I waited for the others while the sun sank behind the mountain. After half an hour Milo and Rubina arrived, in his car. Then the others, dribbling in.

It was supposed to be only a rehearsal, it became our end of summer concert. We put up flyers announcing it in the stores in the town square and along the avenue. I put one up in the waiting room of my office. To some it seemed strange, the chorus singing at Dente del Lupo. Milo, however, was immediately enthusiastic about my proposal. Pierluigi the tenor arranged some lights. I have no idea if anyone will come up to hear us. The people in the town don't appreciate new things, but sometimes I'm surprised.

I thought the chorus members would be dressed for the mountain, and yet we're all elegant, in black, as at the other concerts. Samira tries out her voice, around her throat a scarf with glittering spangles. A holly leaf pricks her bare ankle under the skirt.

184 · DONATELLA DI PIETRANTONIO

Cars start arriving, park in a line along the road. I can hardly believe I'm seeing them walking toward us, some with their phone flashlights on. The space fills up. We get ready to start, the audience sits on the ground, some remain standing. The Sheriff hesitates: increasingly heavy, she doesn't know where to settle. Then Doralice joins her, takes her by the arm and guides her. She has the slenderness of twenty, that trust in her gaze. She helps her mother sit down on a rock, then leaves her and comes forward. She sits on the grass, legs crossed, a rebel lock over her face. She greets me with just a glance: Hey, Lucia. Nodding almost imperceptibly she indicates Ciarango, a little apart, tying his horse to a beech. He, too, is present—our cowboy.

Now we're really ready, in a moment Milo will give us the opening beat. And there's my father, too, at the back, in the NAVIGARE shirt, with a heavier shirt hanging from his crossed arms. He looks at me and pretends he's not. Osvaldo taps him on the back and he turns. It's a moment, already they're going off together, talking.

Samira's voice rises, alone and proud in the first lines. Then we follow her in *Ederlezi*, with her we chant the feast and sacrifice of the lamb. Summoned by the music, Tania and Virginia emerge from the darkest part of the woods, cross the meadow lightly. Milo doesn't even notice as they pass behind him. They sit beside Doralice, Tania with the jade necklace on her chest. They listen smiling. *A me čorolo, dural besava /amaro dive, Ederlezi* (But me, poor me, I am sitting apart/Our day, Ederlezi) . . . Their tent isn't far, they've got everything ready so they can leave early tomorrow morning. The chorus tonight is a surprise, breaks the silence of years. The last summer star shoots across the sky over Dente del Lupo.

Donatella Di Pietrantonio lives in Penne, Abruzzo, where she practices as a pediatric dentist.

A Girl Returned, her third novel, won the Campiello Prize. *A Sister's Story* was a finalist for the 2021 Strega Prize and a New Yorker Best Book of 2022. *The Brittle Age* won the Strega Prize in 2024.